The Magicians: Omnibus 4 –
Darkness Within

by Rachel Lawson

As written on website AllPoetry.com
https://allpoetry.com/Rachel_Lawson

The Devil's Nightmare

"So your name is Lancelot, it is a rather pretentious name!" said Orlando King, the new employer of Lance Alexander who wore a business suit.

"I'm called Lance," said Lance trying not to insult his boss by saying King was too.

"What did you do for a job before this," asked Lando.

"I was a stage hypnotist, in a solo act, since my sister died," said Lance quietly.

"Wasn't she murdered?" Lando asked.

"I'd rather not talk about it," Lance told him.

"How did it happen?" Lando said.

"I don't want to talk about it," Lance said.

"Tell me!" demanded Lando coldly.

"Ok you ghoul! She and her husband were shot and autopsied by a mad alien-hating scientist on a whim!" shouted Lance crying both angry and sad.

"That will make a good story write it!" Lando ordered.

"No!" said Lance refusing.

"No matter I'll get someone else to write it!" said Lando offhandedly.

"You have no heart!" Lance said crying.

"No, I can't afford one bad for business," said Lando "you will learn it if you stay this bloodthirsty business for as long as I have."

"I have a heart!" Lance thought, "and have been in bloodier business than you!"

"Maybe," Lance said.

"Mercy!" cried a man at the end of Lance's sword later that day.

"Mercy? you want mercy you slaughtered my sister and her husband," said Lance who had finally caught up with their killer who was stalking Lance as an alien he thought might be a good subject for an experiment and autopsy.

"I'll let you go!" said the scientist.

"You chose the wrong victim," said Lance.

"I see that! I won't tell anyone about you Enchanter," said the scientist.

"Who is the Enchanter? I am the Necromancer, son of the King of the grim reapers, avenger of Fate! You can't kill me!" Lance said his eyes burning with hate.

"Necromancer! Oh god no!" said the scientist.

"I shall avenge all you victims human and otherwise!" said Lance raised his sword and it fell.

"Oh Lance there you are!" Lando said walking in the room seeing Lance holding the bloody sword hovering over the body.

"Lando!" Lance said in horror.

"What have we here!" said Lando rubbing his hands.

Lance stood stunned with no idea what to do.

"You did not see this! You were never here!" Lance said instinctively.

"Are you mad I can see you don't try your tricks on me Enchanter!" said Lando coldly.

"Enchanter you know who I am?" Lance said bewildered.

The Enchanter was a secretive local Superhero who worked with the police.

"He tried to murder me!" said Lance.

"Who has the bloody sword?" said Lando amused at Lance discomfort.

"Will you tell the Police what you found?" asked Lance.

"Tempting, but not I will if you don't do what I ask you to do!" said Lando knowing the Enchanter would make a good reporter for the paper.

"So this is blackmail!" said Lance reading Lando's mind.

"Yes," said Lando.

The Chicken Virus

"Achoo!" Went the Masked Chicken sneezing in his friend the coroner Blake Alexander's face.

"Thanks for that Gabriel!" Blake said angrily, "I don't need corona virus!"

"Don't worry I just have hay fever!" said the chicken.

"Careful dad he'll give you the chicken virus!" Lance, Blake's son said walking up to them keeping his distance.

"That is what I'm afraid off he was over seas last week and came back from there when corona hit. He could have caught it!" Blake grumbled.

"You do know you are meant to be in quarantine at home Gabriel," Lance said.

"I tried I got bored!" said the Chicken.

"Watch TV, read a book!" Blake said.

"I read Good Omens and watched the show on Amazon Prime was good but the show ended so I came here" said the Chicken

"That may not be hay fever it could be the corona virus," said Lance.

"What do think doc?" chirped the chicken.

"Don't call me doc! You should be tested!" said Blake.

"No need corona can't kill us we aren't human!" said the chicken.

"But you can spread the virus and it kills people!" said Blake.

"Yeah but it won't kill me!" The Chicken said.

"God! You sound like young person I saw on TV! The virus won't stop you socializing because it won't hurt you!" Blake said amazed how selfish the Chicken was. Blake stormed off in disgust trying to not call The Chicken rude names to his face.

"Looks like friend Blake is in a bit of a bad mood." said the chicken.

"What do you expect some of his best friends are old humans," Lance said.

"I forget how old he is 1000 and something," said the Chicken.

"1100 next June," Lance said.

"Oh old! how old are you," The chicken said.

" A little Younger!" said the true millennial Lance.

A week Later in the local morgue which was located a small nearby hospital's basement.
Blake lifted a surgical knife about to do an incision in to a corpse. Blake sneezed he ended up stabbing the corpse in the heart.
At that moment in the room walked Lance seeing him stabbing the body.

"He not dead enough or didn't you like him?" Asked Lance.

" No I sneezed, I'll have hell to pay when Dante finds out what happens!" said Blake.

"He's your assistant not your boss!" said Lance.

Blake coughed in his handkerchief and honked his nose.

"I think you may have caught the chicken virus you should be at home!" said Lance.

"I'll see the doctor when I can see if I can do a test!" Blake said.

Later that week.

In a small dingy little wooden office Blake sat doing paperwork.

He sneezed and knocked over his bottle of ink all over the paper work.

"D-" said Blake about to swear interrupted by from his thoughts by his assistant arriving. "ante! Don't!"

"How could you! You ruined it!" Dante said having a fit.

"I didn't do it on purpose? I sneezed and knocked it" Blake said.

"How could you it is the most important paperwork-" Dante shouted.

"It's only a few death records!" said Blake wanting to kick himself for sneezing.

"They are reaper filed not photocopies of coroner's files!"said Dante. Who was trying to wipe the ink off only making it worse.

Blake had a bad coughing fit.

"Are you alright?" asked Dante.

"I caught the Chicken virus!" Blake said.

"The What?: asked Dante.

"I caught corona virus off the Chicken. They had to lock him up to go in quarantine he was spreading the virus at the police station!" Blake said.

"Why are you here? You should be in quarantine yourself!" said Dante.

"I am I'm working from home!" said Blake.

"Home! Home! You call this home I call this Hell!" said Dante.

"It's not that bad and it's in my backyard!" Blake said.

"Aren't you afraid of making people sick?" Dante said.

"In the afterlife? No only the dead here and the dead can't get sick!" said Blake.

"Then how are you sick?" asked the exasperated Dante.

"My body is sick so my soul is also ill!" Blake said.

There was a terrifying scream outside the office.

Blake and Dante left the office to investigate.

A grim reaper was hovering around a fear struck man.

"Necromancer what is he doing here?" asked Blake.

The reaper turned to them..

"He tried to rob your home dad went in the backyard and got lost here he's been here for a week!" The reaper said.

"Who are you thief?" asked Blake.

"Nutbean, John Nutbean! Mr Grim reaper!" said the thief scared seeing Blake and Dante as they were then a pair of grim reapers.

Lance was the reaper, the Necromancer.

"What will we do with this fish!" asked the Necromancer.

"Throw him back in the water!" Blake said a swirling portal appeared and Blake said " step Into the portal Nutbean!"

Nutbean felt compelled to do it and he disappeared with the portal.

"Oh! Him he's fine he is in another part of town lost and terrifies." said Blake.

"He won't talk!" Lance said laughing.

Lance sneezed.

"Bless you!" said Blake.

They all laughed.

Queen of Vampires

The queen of vampires got a picture painted by a friend,
she looked at it at it's end,
It was worse that she could imagine it was a picture of her in hell,
the artist was the Masked Chicken he hated her what could she expect? Oh well!

Xenophobia or The Fear of Strangers

"Hello ladies and gentlemen I am Blake Fire and he is Max Starfire welcome to our magic show,"
said Blake Alexander on the stage of his popular magic show.
"Go back to where you came from aliens we don't need or want you on Earth!" shout a man in the
audience.
"We were born on Earth like you," Max Starfire who was half human said to the heckler.
"You're aliens!" shouted back the heckler.
"No we aren't human that's your problem with us!" said Blake.
"Go back to where you came from! aliens you don't belong on earth" shouted the heckler.
"We have lived on earth longer than your kind you are descended from him," Blake said.
"Yeah right pull the other leg it falls off!" the heckler shouted.
"Front of house can do your job and show the heckler out!" Max said.
The heckler was dragged out calling them bad things and the ushers traitors to their planet and their
people.

Dark Angel or The Visitation

Astra Starfire, the Queen of Vampires once visited her parents' grave. She stood in front of a stone
angel a top a grave in the cemetery crying her mascara ran from her eyes she looked like a dark
angel to her husband Max who stood in front of her. In her hand a red rose a petal fell blown off by
the winds of Autumn. Dead leaves from near by trees fall. She placed the rose on their grave the
legend on it was engraved in red on a black marker stone which read Valkira Laura Merlin and
Alexander Saphirus Merlin know as the Dark Angel and the Dark Sorcerer, dearly beloved parents
to Astra.

The Necromantrix's Lament

Fate and life
hate and death,
blood runs off my sword,
another life ends,
regret and fear,
will I be caught,
did I do right,
I sit beneath cold the moon holding my sword,
I am falling apart,
I am told I do right.
taking lives of rogues,
I wonder are they right,
are they wrong,
do I do wrong,
does their sin make my sin a virtue?
am I mad?
all I know is I'm confused and sad.

Rogue of Honor or The Assasin

A tall handsome man in a black shirt and pants with glasses sat in his dingy little office. He was
scribbling on papers with some skill with a black quill and ink. He stopped when he heard his son
Lance arguing with his assistant outside the office loudly.
"Go away Necromancer he's working!" Blake Alexander heard his assistant shouting. "But I have to
see him it is important!" Lance shouted back. Blake got up walked to the door and opened it
standing in the door way he asked why they were arguing.
"He wanted to disturb you from your important work," Dante, Blake's assistant said. Lance glared at
Dante.
"But this is important!" said Lance.
"Not as important as his work!" said Dante, "He must run a smooth consistent office for this place
to keep out of anarchy."
"Dante takes my job more seriously than I do! What is wrong, boy?" said Blake.
"Someone tried to assassinate the King of the Earth," said Lance.
"They did how is Granddad?" asked Blake worried.
"He's alive! He was lucky he was just winged," Lance said.
"I told him it was not important! Nobody died!" Dante said..
"So it was not important," said Blake, the Emperor of the grim reapers and the Underworld among

other things.

"Where is he?" asked Blake.

"Charing Cross Hospital under police guard. That is not all I came to say Fate has decreed that I am to kill the assassin," said Lance.

"Oh? Do we know who they are?" asked Blake curiously.

"That's the problem we don't," said Lance sadly.

"We'd better go see my Granddad and find out how he is and what he knows?" Blake said.

"No you have work to do Blake!" said Dante.

"No I have to see the King of the Earth!" said Blake standing up to Dante who was a a bit of a pen pusher and took Blake's job too seriously.

"What's so important about the King of the Earth?" said Dante who didn't know the King of the Earth's secret. The man known as the King of the Earth was in reality more than that. He was not really Fred Alexander a lowly planetary King. He was actually more better known as Sapphirus Argent, emperor of the silver intergalactic empire. It consisted of the entire galaxy.

He just preferred the name Fred Alexander his human name. As Sapphirus Argent sounded too stuffy for him. Most of his family had two names a human name and an alien name. All but Lazulite Argent the last fate who reigned as ruler of everything. He was a bit of a busy body with a dark streak. He made Lance play avenging angel killing bad guys. The police saw him as a mad serial killer as did Blake. He was not mad just misguided and Blake knew it. Lazulite went by his lofty surname Argent.

"Let's go see the King now," said Blake.

"Beat you there!" said Lance disappearing in to thin air follow by his dad who disappeared too. Leaving one angry Dante alone.

Blake and Lance appeared at the reception desk of the hospital.

"What do you want Dr Death," a man Blake knew only too well said he was an orderly.

"No not you! Where is the receptionist?" said Blake rolling his eyes.

"On a break I'm filling in!" said the rude orderly.

"Ok! where is Frederick Alexander's room?" asked Blake.

"You aren't needed there! He's alive!" said the orderly curtly.

"I know I came to see him he is my grandfather!" said Blake.

"He can't be he's as old as you are!" said the orderly.

"No! We just look young for our age," Blake said.

"And I suppose he's your son then!" said the orderly pointing at Lance who looked 25 too.

"As a matter of fact he is," said Blake.

"Yeah right pull the other leg it's a corpse," said the Orderly.

"Oh! never mind just tell me where Fred is!" huffed Blake.

"I'll take you there," said the Orderly smelling something fishy.

"Ok! Lead the way, Mr Jack Taylor! said Lance reading the orderly's name badge.

"Are you an actor I think I met you at a friend's show?" asked Lance as they walked.

"Yes who's your friend," asked Jack.

"Argent," said Lance.

"Yes I know him bossy fellow," said Jack.

"Yes," said Lance.

"Fred Alexander is in here!" said Jack as they got to the room Fred was in.

"Do you know these men?" asked the Orderly.

"Yes! Hi Blake! Hi Lance!" said Fred who was in a hospital bed. He was under the guard of a Policeman in odd clothes. He wore a red tux and top hat and was masked. "Are you one of them Magicians?" asked Jack seeing to police man. The Magicians were alien super heroes who helped out the police.

"Yes," said Blake, Lance, Fred and the man in red at the same time.

"I was talking to him," said Jack pointing at the man in red.

"Hi Uncle Reynard." said Blake to his great uncle the man in red.

"Hello Blake! Hello Lancelot! I was just asking the king here about his shooter," said Rey, who was Fred's brother.

"King? what he is king of?" asked Jack.

""I'm king of the world," Fred said awkwardly hoping not to sound too pretentious.

"The world? What world," Jack asked

"This world, the earth of course!" said Rey who laughed at the thought anyone would need to ask.

"He's one of your kind!" asked Jack.

"He's my brother, The Red Fox, the King of Mars," said Fred.

"Then you two are related to him!" said the Orderly.

"Like I said," Blake said.

"Oh I can't take this?"said Jack wandering off.

"How are you granddad?" asked Blake.

"Fine! Just can't write!" said Fred.

"Hi," said Lance.

"Did you see who shot you?" Blake asked.

"Not well, I think he had grey skin," said Fred.

"Not human then," said Lance.

"Of course not boy how many humans have grey skin!" said Blake.

"Any more clues," asked Lance ignoring his dad's comment.

"He called me by my name?" Fred said.

"King of the Earth or Fred Alexander," asked Rey.

"My real name!" said Fred looking around suspiciously for people who may hear him.

"You mean the used your Imperial name" said Rey in a quiet voice.

"Yes! They said something about ridding the empire of the tyrant, Sapphirus Argent," said Fred quietly.

Lance closed the door to the room.

"It seems related to the intergalactic summit we are holding here no one else would call you that," said Blake.

"Yes put on a summit and wackos usually come out of the floorboards!" Lance said.

"Yes," said Blake.

"He's going to try again," said Blake.

"Yes more than likely at the summit! So we'll have to cancel it," said Rey.

"We can trap him in the act!" said Lance.

"No we can't risk the life of the Emperor!" said Rey.

"You aren't the only one who wants to get the assassin. According to Mortimer said his son the Necromancer wants to kill the assassin!" said Blake. Who was secretly Mortimer which was his reaper name. Which neither Rey or Fred knew was anything more than a friend to Blake.

"Does he?" said Lance, "Maybe we can trap him or draw him out or the Necromancer can kill the assassin if we don't cancel it,"

"True!" said Rey, "but I don't know which assassin I would put my money on."

Days later Fred stood by a podium with his arm looking normal. His bandages were hidden beneath a silver tux with blue trim. "Welcome to the Intergalactic conference of the Silver empire. I am Sapphirus Argent, Emperor of the silver intergalactic empire." said Fred to the people in the summit into a microphone.

"Hale Sapphirus!" Voices shouted from the crowd. Behind Sapphiru stood: his son, Dark Star or Variscite Argent, other wise known as Valentine Alexender, he was Blake's dad.

the Raven or Variscite's wife Larimar know as Laura Alexander. Blake's aunt Sapphira Merlin was there.

Blue Midnight, Emperor of the local solar system or Alexandrite Argent who we know as Blake Alexander.

Blake's wife Anatase Argent called Angela Alexander by humans. Lastly was The Enchanter or Lakelandite Argent we know as Lancelot Alexander.

"I would like to thank my Grandson. The local emperor Alexandrite for organizing this summit. I would also like to thank my brother Rhodonite for organizing the security."

Later in the summit there was masquerade dance. Lance wandered around looking for for suspicious characters and actions.

While he was looking around he found 2 suspicious characters. They were his niece Astra Sapphira Starfire and her husband Maximilien or Marcasite Starfire. They were the vampire King and Queen. Lance raised Astra when her parents were murdered. He was like a father to her.

"Hi Lance have you found him yet?" asked Max, who like his wife knew Lance and Blake were Mortimer and the Necromancer .

"Not yet the night is still young you are the most suspicious people I met here!" said Lance.

"No one more suspicious than little old us?" joked Astra.

Lance wandered off leaving them to themselves.

Astra queen of vampires went to a masquerade,
opportunist, she was with her husband Max, the king,
they danced all night, then they got people alone and they
took a little drink
She savored the taste of the blood she drank,
she drank it in a wine glass in her black-gloved hand. Her gloves were of fish net lace her hands bejeweled.
her husband stood admiring her long black tresses, her dress, and
her gothic beauty,
Her mask a black lace mask fit tight on her finely chiseled face. Max told a joke. She laughed and cried she laughed too much. She flirting with silence bit her fingertips. They danced like newlyweds enjoying the dance and each other's company. Their eyes never left each other It was as if nothing else mattered, their hearts in their mouths, the world felt like as if it was theirs alone. They took joy in each other's touch and movements and the other's loving glance. The world was lost all that existed was the music and the magical moment which lasted till the dawn's light peaked in and the moment was gone

Back to Lance he was still wandering around when his father walked over to him.

"Hi boy have you seen anything suspicious?" said Blake.

"Hi Dad the only suspicious thing I've seen is vampires. I think you will have a vampire victim or 2 in your morgue tomorrow as coroner." Lance joked darkly.

"I have no doubt of that!" said Blake grimly.

Rey seeing them wandered over to them and asked them if they saw anything suspicious.

"Nothing unusual just X-Zeraciens getting drunk on the punch think some body spiked it!" said Lance.

"It seems so!" said Blake.

"I wonder if the Necromancer is here?" said Rey.

"I don't know here or there I suppose, he could be anyone or anywhere, right Lance," joked Blake.

"I wouldn't know," said Lance offhandedly.

"Look whose coming," said Blake seeing Fred walking up to them.

"Oh damn the Sycophants!" said Lance under his breath.

"How is everybody tonight." asked Fred greeting them warmly he was happy to see them.

"Good granddad," Blake said.

"All is good with me too," said Lance.

" Good! How are you?" Rey said.

"Just working out deals with the ambassadors," said Fred.

Fred was not alone he was surrounded by a gaggle of delegates.

"Are they the people from behind you when you opened the summit?" an ambassador said recognizing them..

"This is my grandson the emperor of this solar system Blue Midnight and the Enchanter. He is his eldest son and he is my brother Rhodonite, the Martian King." said Fred to his followers.

"Alexandrite Argent and your son here Lakelandite Argent. Your other son Chrysoprase, the Time Keeper is amazing. Please tell me what happened to your daughter. I have heard a lot about your family, Alexandrite!" a grey X-Zeracien aliens said shaking Blake's arm not quite getting the greeting of hand shaking right.

"Nice to meet you," said Blake smiling charmingly. He ignored the mistake and the reference to his murdered daughter which was still raw even 20 years later. Lance smiled "kakna es nar nesh," Lance said to the alien in it's own language. Roughly translating as "Good evening I have to go see you around!" and walked away to look for something out of place that was just a sycophantic ambassador. He was no trouble just a pain in the neck to Lance. Who despised sycophants more than pen pushers he had no time for either of them.

He knew sycophants annoyed his father as much as he did but he could take it because he was a pen pusher.

A teenage girl walked up to him.

"This is the most boring party I've ever seen!" said the teenager.

"This is a political party Chrysoberyl it is meant to be boring," Lance said.

"Stop using my real name call me Kristine!" said Chrysoberyl.

"Sorry Kristine! have you seen any thing strange tonight?" Lance asked her she was his daughter and apprentice. She had been looking for suspicious things there at the masquerade.

"Oh yeah I saw Astra and Max killing someone and drinking their blood out of wine glasses. yuck!" said Kristine.

"Oh? Other than that!" Lance said to his daughter.

"Yeah!" Kristine said.

"What did you see?" asked Lance.

"Oh! I saw a grey alien looking very suspicious he was dressed as Zorro." Kristine said.

"Haven't I told you don't be racist call them by their proper name X-Zeraciens not by their skin color! lectured Lance.

"Dad!" Kristine protested.

"What was it doing?" asked Lance.

"Fighting with a Venusian bartender over his wearing a weapon!" said Kristine.

"What a sword?" asked Lance laughing.

"No a gun." said Kristine.

"A gun? where is he now?" asked Lance panicking.

"He's talking to Granddad," said Kristine pointing at an oddly dress gray alien.

Lance ran over to them.

"Dad it's him!" said Lance in his dad's mind, as he grabbed the arm of Zorro. Lance dragged Zorro into another room.

It was all set up for a banquet it was empty. The sounds outside the room leaked in the room. laughter and music rang slightly muffled into the room. Lance and the alien Zorro ignored it. "Who are you and why are you as you people say man handling me?" Zorro demanded.

"The last person you will see alive!" said Lance darkly.

"Who are you?" demanded the alien.

"I know who you are and why you are here!" Lance said

"I doubt that!" said the alien.

"You have come to kill the emperor Sapphirus and I have come to kill you!" said Lance

"Who are you?" asked the alien.

"No one you need to know!" said Lance.

The alien was trying to pull away but he wasn't strong enough.

"Let me go or I'll shoot you!" said the alien.

Lance looked at the alien and saw a gun in it's free hand.

He let the alien go it backed off aiming the gun at Lance.

Lance looked angry with himself for not thinking of the gun.

The alien ran out of the room. Lance picked up a knife and followed it.

There were murmurs outside of the room. the alien screamed "Ji fe ne Argent!" and there was gun shot.

Fred fell and Lance raised his hand the knife was gone. It was in the aliens back. Blake helped his granddad who he knocked over seeing the gun. Rey ran to see if his brother was alright.

He saw Fred was just shocked but fine. So he ran to the alien. He was dead.

"Lance what happened?" asked Rey.

"I killed him! He was trying to shoot the emperor of the galaxy!" Lance said.

"Good work Lance! I knew the Necromancer would fail to kill him!" said Rey

Blake looked at Lance and bowed his head knowingly. Acknowledging that the Necromancer did good.

The Enchanter and Chimera (short story)

Sir Lancelot of the Lake, was an enchanter.

He was a mysterious man of alien royal blood.

He longer than most mortal men did live.

He once in knightly days travelled the lands of the Arabian knights of old.

A roving knight was he back then.

He heard of a giant bird of the days of yore menacing the lands there.

"How can It be?" did Sir Lancelot proclaim because the bird existed never.

"I will slay it to save the people of the land," he said and went to Arabia in a flash of light.

He appeared in a wadi in Arabia near the home of the great bird of prey.

"There be the Roc?" cried Sir Lancelot when the bird was in sight.

"It's not natural, it is a creature of magic I sense!" said the knight.

"I cannot fly like a bird, it is a creature of the wing. So a creature of the wing I need," muttered the enchanter to himself.

A great creature he devised.

A chimera of lion and bird it was.

It roared like the winds of the desert.

He sat upon his steeds back.

"Fly!" Sir Lancelot roared. The chimera flew aloft and he did soar through the clouds.

The chimera's wings losing feathers as he flew.

The knight in armour sat watching his foe.

He lifted his enchanted sword from his sword belt.

He watched the great bird for a moment.

"Go to the Bird!" cried the knight.

The chimera flew towards the Roc.

The bird looked on them as a human would a fly.
The Roc tried to swipe them and knock them from the sky.
To the bird the chimera and his master were small.
The chimera dodged and weaved and missed the bird's claws, wings, and beak some how.
There was a squawk near by the knight distracted saw a nest with a baby Roc chick.
The chimera was knocked to the ground with a thud and clatter of armour.
"Thank god I was in armor!" said the knight picking himself up.
The chimera was injured.
Sir Lancelot cast a healing spell.
The chimera was made well again.
The knight sat upon the chimera and up they flew.
They soared close to the Roc and the knight drew his sword slaying the Roc which dropped to the ground dead with a thud.
Then the chimera and his master flew to the nest.
The knight dismounted.
The knight strode on foot to the baby.
It tried to eat him thinking him food.
The knight fell over a human leg bone the remnants of meal of the Rocs.
This startled and spooked the knight.
The bird when it for the kill..
The knight pushed the dead bird off him and his sword and sighed.
He set fire to the nest.
Then he walked back to his steed and flew to the ground and set fire to the mother.
"Ashes to ashes dust to dust!" said the knight over it and the chimera melted out of existence. In flash of light the knight was gone.

The Enchanter and Chimera (poem)

In knightly days of yore did the Enchanter create a chimera creature,
A hybrid of lion and bird to hunt a giant Roc bird,
A giant bird of prey of the lands of Arabia years of old,
He admired the Roc as it gracefully flew through the clouds from the back of his Chimera
He wore a suit of shining armour, feathers flew from his steed's giant wings,
He drew his enchanted sword and the flying lion flew in for the kill,
He stabbed the snapping giant bird and it fell from the sky,
Landing in a great thud.

Life Beyond Death

"Hello Hope, welcome to the afterlife." said the emperor of the grim reapers greeting his dead 1st wife's mother's ghost. They were in his dingy little office in the other world.

"Blake? Angela? what are you 2 doing here?" asked the ghost of his mother-in-law.

Some men would have enjoyed the meeting, having their mother-in-law dead. Blake was not happy nor was his new wife who was his first wife reincarnated by Fate. "Blake broke the rules for me. He is the emperor of the underworld. I am not supposed to be here but I had to say my goodbyes," said Blake's 2nd wife Angela.

"Oh! that's nice of you Blake," said Hope.

"We don't have long Fate is coming soon!" said Blake, "I'll wait outside!" Who left them to talk alone.

Moments later Angel burst out the room in tears.

"Angel what is wrong?" asked Blake embracing her.

"Mum!" said Angela sobbing.

"What?" asked Blake moving away from her and dashing to the door.

He opened it to find Hope was gone.

Angel what happened," Blake asked his wife.

"We were talking and she suddenly disappeared like she was teleporting and she was gone!" said Angela who had followed him.

"That is impossible!" said Blake, "I know a man who can explain this!"

A dark portal opened.

"Come with me Angel," said Blake they entered the portal.

the appeared in the halls of time a place out of time, out of space, out of that dimension.

"Hello mum and dad I was waiting for you." said a man who lived there. He was the immortal alien known as the Timekeeper. Who saw future and past in a pond like a gypsy would a crystal ball.

"Hello boy!" Blake said.

"Where is she?" asked the still crying Angela.

"She's fine!" said the Timekeeper looking worried.

"How?" said Blake.

"She is alive and well again!" said the Timekeeper.

"Alive? How did fate reincarnate her?" asked Blake.

"No." said the Timekeeper.

"Then who and how?" Asked Blake.

"The Necromancer brought her body back to life!" said Tempus, the Timekeeper.

"Lance? Why?" asked Angela confused.

"He did it for you, mum he knew how much you missed her like dad did," said Tempus

"What is wrong then I know that look?" said Angela.

"She lives again!" said Tempus.

"Why is that wrong?" asked his mother.

"Her death was meant to be!" said Tempus.

"Oh! Another fixed point in time eh?" Blake said.

"Yes!" said Tempus.

"What do we do now?" asked Blake.

"You need to go back in time and stop him bringing her back," said Tempus not wanting to say it.

"Why can't she live?" asked Angela devastated at the thought of losing her mum again.

"Time will be broken I saw!" said Tempus.

"What does that mean?" asked Angela.

"All time has become one moment after the break we have been sheltered here. All things are occurring in one moment now." said Tempus.

"Oh!" Blake said wondering if he was lying.

"Look in the pool of time to see I'm not lying dad," said Tempus reading his dad's mind.

in the pool all they saw was a billion things occurring in that moment including the end of existence.

"Oh my god!" Angela said seeing it.

"You see!" said Tempus.

"We do!" Blake said aghast.

"Take the portal over there," said Tempus pointing out one of a million.

Blake lead the way.

"I wish we didn't have to do this?" Angela said as she and Blake stepped in the portal.

"Me too," said Tempus angrily splashing the water of the pool of time when they were gone.

"Lance!" cried Angel seeing her son the Necromancer. He was kneeling cradling her mother's head off the ground by her grave.

"Mum?" said Lance not sure why she was there.

"Boy don't do it!" Blake shouted.

"Don't do what?" asked Lance.

"Bring her back!" Blake said.

"You don't want the paperwork deal with it!" said Lance who saw his dad as a pen pusher.

"No!" snapped Blake.

"That is all it is paperwork nothing more!" Lance said frustrated.

"No! No! Don't bring her back!" pleaded Angela.

"I'm doing it for you!" said Lance.

"I know but we must let her go!" Angela said walking to him.

"We are all mortal we only appear immortal! We can't bring back all we lose without unwanted side effects!" said Blake.

Angela knelt to her son's level.

"Let her go!" said Angela.

Lance dropped his grandmother's lifeless body and burst into tears.

Angela hugged him.

"Angel!" 5 minutes later after Lance had left Blake said , "We have to go back!"

She looked in her mum's face one last time and whispered "Goodbye!"

to her and cast a spell reburying her.

Then they stepped into a portal and were gone. Through cool and crisp air of the night rang the hoot of an owl. The moon shone down like silver on the grave of Hope. There was a new inscription on it glowing like silver in the light "She will live on beyond her death in heaven."

The Mortuary of Shadows

"Blake He's not trying to steal your job!" the wife of Coroner Blake Alexander told her husband. He had just told her his new co- worker in the morgue was trying to steal his job. "Angel he's just too perfect!" moaned Blake, " I can't keep up!" In the room walked the man who they were talking about they were at work in Blake's dingy little office in the morgue. "What do you want Dante?" asked Blake.

"I wanted to tell you I stayed back a little last night. I did all the autopsies and the paperwork for them and found a better way to do a few things. I'll show you later," said Dante Drax. "You did 10 autopsies and the paperwork!" Blake said exasperated. "I did something wrong?" asked Dante asked Blake not sure why he was asking him it. In the room appeared a man in a police sergeants uniform out of thin air. "Hi Uncle Rey what's up?" said Blake. " Hi Blake I need help on a case," said the Sergeant who was not as human as he looked. "I have plenty of time Dante did all the work here!" said Blake. "Oh good I actually came here to see Dante!" Reynard Xander- Drax said. "Oh what do you need?" asked Dante. "A coroner It's a murder!" said Reynard. Blake was put out he rolled his eyes and looked his wife in the eyes. Blake had been Reynard's go to man when he needed help on a case. His wife smiled at him. "Angela I'll need your assistance," said Dante to Angela who was an assistant coroner. "Ok!" said Angela. Blake sat alone and bored listening to Cold Play music on his phone. He did this until his least favourite person came. "We got some work for you Dr Death!" said the Orderly. "Ok what is it?" yawned Blake stretching. The Orderly gave him a folder Blake read through it and turned off his phone. "Take me to them!" said Blake rising from his chair. The Orderly led Blake up stairs to a group of worried people. "Them!" the Orderly said and walked off. "What about us?" asked an elderly man. "You are here for Henry Walters. "Yes! Why how did the operation go?" asked John his Dad. "Sadly I'm afraid he didn't make it sorry!" Blake said. "Oh no!" the Mother of Henry Walters cried. "How it was just a tooth extraction!" said Mr Walters confused. "I think it was the anaesthetic. It can have a bad reaction in some people!" said Blake feeling like a ghoul for enjoying the distraction which this grim work was. "Oh!" said Mr Walters. Later a dimension away. "What do you mean? I have another assistant? I never had anyone but Morton!" said Mortimer the lord of the underworld in his surprisingly well made old wood lined office. In the the office was nothing but a old chair and wooden desk filled with towers of paperwork. on the desk sat a quill and ink also in the room was a door to a capacious closet. "Ok show them in," Mortimer said. When the assistant walked in Mortimer Muttered "Oh Hell!" The assistant was floored too. "Blake you were the last man I expected to see here!" said Dante Drax. "I take it he knows you in the other world Dad," said the reaper known by the name of the Necromancer. "Yes he works in the morgue?" said Blake who was Mortimer. "The morgue?" said the Necromancer. "He's a coroner too!" said Blake awkwardly. "So that's your place with the interdimensional portal to here in the backyard I came here through," said Dante "I did some weeding before I came here there!". "Yes," said Blake disturbed by the fact Dante had done his garden work. "I'll help you with your paperwork!" said Dante. "Darn!" Blake thought. he thought he would be replaced there too, "What wrong Dad?" asked the Necromancer in his father's head. "Nothing," Blake replied in his son's head "Ok you don't want to talk of it," said the Necromancer. thinking he wasn't interested anyway. He never did like meddling in others business.

Later that week Blake sat boredly. Practising throwing red back Bicycle brand poker cards across the room into a blue top hat on the other side of the room mostly accurately. Somewhere in under world in his office. The paper work was all gone Dante had done it all to Blake's annoyance. Blake pulled out his phone and said "Ok Google Play Cold Play!" "Death And All His Friends" played Blake looked depressed. the cards disappeared into thin air. In walked Dante. "Don't you ever knock?" asked Blake. "No it wastes time!" said Dante. "What do you want?" asked Blake. "I thought I should take death away from his friends for a while," said Dante. "What something else are you planing to out do me in something else" said Blake depressed. "You are so depressed and lifeless at the moment Blake you need to do some work to brighten you up!" said Dante. "What can I do you've done everything already," said Blake. Dante picked up the hat and dusted it off and passed to Blake. "You mean Blue Midnight can help!" said Blake. "Yes there is always work for my Emperor Blue Midnight!" said Dante smiling.

"What do I call you in that disguise?" asked Blake of Dante who was dressed as a masked magician in yellow. "Starlight!" said Dante the police call me the Starlight Knight," said Dante. "Isn't that an anime character's name?" Said Blake an eyebrow raising beneath his own blue mask. "Yes, I like the name," said Dante. as they walked to the reception area at the local police station. "Blue Midnight and the Starlight Knight hello what do you want?" a receptionist asked. "We are here to see my Uncle," said Blake tilting his blue top hat on his head. "Ok come inside I'll tell him your coming?" the receptionist said. "Thanks!" said Blake and they opened the door to the hub of the station where police men and women were working and walking about to go here and there. Blake saw a police woman looking a bit annoyed Blake wondered why. As they walked past her Blake a hand hit Blake's back. :"Blue Midnight hi!" a man said. "Chicken!" Blake said he didn't need this meeting. Blake turned around to see a man dress in a yellow feathered chicken outfit with a mask.

"Yes! I was trying to ask the lady if I could work on a case with the police me being a superhero like you and the knight here." said the Masked Chicken, "So far she says no!" The Mask Chicken is a hero, his saves run to zero, he's actually a serial pest, even if he does his best, he gets in the the way, he never saves the day. "I wonder why you are a nice guy," said Blake being nice. "I'll wear her down, you'll see!" said the Chicken. "Good Luck Gabriel," said Blake to the Chicken. Blake looked apologetically at the police woman. "Have a good day, Blake," said the Chicken as Blake and Dante started to walk off. "You too my friend," said Blake glad to get away from him. They walked to the sergeant's office and Blake knocked. Dante just walked in. "Come in Blake called," Blake's Uncle. Blake walked in. "Do you have any work for a bored coroner?" asked Dante. "Why?" Rey asked, "I caught him sitting in his office alone doing nothing but listening to music and reeking of boredom," said Dante. "Oh," said Rey who then laughed. Rey shuffled through his folders on his desk looking at them and stood up and gave one to Blake. "Paperwork!" Blake said surprised how much he missed paperwork he generally hated it. Blake read the pages in folder. "It's him again!" Blake said. "Yes we think the Necromancer did it too," said Rey, "we'll catch him one day." "He doesn't a have snowflake's chance in hell, Hey Blake!" Dante said in Blake's mind. "He'll never arrest my son," Blake said in Dante's head. "I'll take the case!" Blake said aloud. "Mind if I assist you I may be able to help?" asked Dante. "Ok," said Blake Later in the Morgue. "As you know we seldom have any records the victims of the Necromancer except for these letters from hell!" said Blake holding a letter from his son to the police stating the crimes for which they died for. "Can the id him from his writing?" asked Dante. "No he used an enchanted quill and ink." Blake said shaking his head. "Oh so they are literally letters from hell!" chuckled Dante. "Yes," said Blake smiling. In the office walked a tall beard man who resembled Blake. "Hi Dad, Dante," said the Necromancer. "Hi boy! How you someone else!" asked Blake quizzically. "No!" the Necromancer laughed "Give you clues!" "Clues! Have you a death wish?" asked Blake. "No, no, no, of course not!" said the Necromancer "You want to play with your food!" Blake said. "No I want to help you!" said the Necromancer who also wanted to play with the police. "What can you tell us?" asked Dante. "The paper is parchment for the underworld!" said the Necromancer, "the ink is from there too." "Ok, I'll tell them Mortimer told me about it," Blake said "Name Gavin Thompson," said the Necromancer. "Is this how you solve cases usually, Blake?" asked Dante rather impressed. "No this rarely happens!" said Blake. "He needed help so I came to assist." the Necromancer said "He has been in a very dark place for a while so I thought I would help him out of it." "I hope you didn't kill the man to get me out of the dark place," snapped Blake. "No! Of course not! He died because he was an evil serial killer!" said the Necromancer adamantly. "Oh one of you!" hissed Blake, "No I kill for Fate," said the Necromancer. "Whatever you say!" said Blake. A folder materialised on the the empty slab in front of Blake. "What's that?" asked Dante. Blake picked it up an read it's content. "Good work boy It's the other world death certificate! It tells of life death crimes and you redacted the judgement no mortal wants to know of that truth." Blake said. "I'm new to the clerical side of the other world I was a guard," said Dante, "Fate promoted me when helped him on a case!' "Who did you murder for the job?" said Blake. "Ha! Ha!" said the not amused Dante. "He's your boss too!," said the Necromancer. "Nobody I saved an actor from a killer!" said Dante. "Ah! Yes! Fate is an actor too!" said Blake. "Dante you can do the autopsy and and notes for me I'll do the paperwork for the police! snapped Blake. "Ok!" said Dante. "Come boy let's go we need to interview the victim! You take notes as a reaper he won't recognise you!" said Blake leading the Necromancer out of the room and Dante watched them til the door closed and they were gone.

The Manchurian Cadidate

It was a strange day when Blake Alexander found out about this odd case everyone at his hospital wanted to decorate the hospital for Christmas drunk on the Christmas cheer.

but that was nothing the reapers were trying to get the after life business in line with fate's decree that they celebrate Christmas with reapers collecting people as Santa clauses which Blake was totally against. to him it was an anathema. He felt like scrooge It was getting so Christmasy the people at the hospital had stopped calling him Dr Death on the up side but on the down side they called him the Grinch.

he was in a bad mood when he visited the police station which was trimmed for Christmas too.

"We have got some paperwork for you to look at, Blake," said his great uncle the local sergeant of police.

"Great! I love paperwork," said Blake sarcastically he hated paper work.

"know you do that is why we chose you to look at it." said Simon Alexander thinking he was doing Blake a favour

"what is the paperwork for?" asked Blake

"a murder case!" said Simon

"What case?" asked Blake who was a local coroner.

"Tim Wong," said his uncle.

"oh him! the man who reported to us a foreign government tried to hire him as a Manchurian candidate?" Blake said remembering the case.

"Yes that one," said Simon "we suspect a person in the shell company who tried to hire him whose paperwork we confiscated we think they may have paid for a hit man to kill him."

"Who am I working with on this?" asked Blake.

"No one you are on paperwork duty by yourself we know how much you love doing paperwork!" said Simon smiling giving him the paper work in a collection of files.

"Damn!" Blake muttered under his breath.

"I'll leave you to it," Simon said wondering off.

"Blake I got you a present!" the last man Blake wanted to see said putting a fuzzy red Santa hat on Blake's head.

"great thanks Gabriel," said Blake who was so over Christmas.

The man was his lawyer, he was a serial pest because he was an idiot.

"you are welcome, Blake," the man known as the masked chicken said.

"what are you doing?" asked Gabriel Drac, the masked chicken.

"Paperwork!" said Blake

"Need help?" asked the chicken.

"No!" said Blake who knew the chicken would mess it up or get murdered if he helped him.

"Ok! remember I'm here if you need help," said Gabriel who heard a call for help on the police radio.

"I have to go!" said the chicken.

'bye chicken!" said Blake feeling sorry for who ever wanted help. The chicken ran off to the rescue.

"hi dad did the chicken get you too!" said Lance, the superhero the Enchanter. He was Blake's son. Lance wore a blue tux and a mask and a top hat with a Santa hat on it.

"yeah!" Blake said, "he did!"

"I hear you have paperwork to do on the Manchurian candidate murder, you want help with the case, we can split the paperwork?" Lance said.

"As long as no one dies," Blake said to his son who was secretly a serial killer wanted by the police.

"No one will die!" said Lance who only killed people for fate.

"thanks!" Blake said, "I will split it with you we are looking for evidence of a pay off for a hit they think it may be in there!"

later in the realm of the dead in a Gothic dingy office sat a skeleton in a Santa suit reading the paperwork.

there was a knock on the door.

"Come in," the skeleton shouted.

in walked a tall thin human Santa

"hi Blake," said the thin Santa

"hi Argent," the skeleton said.

"I had an idea we should have a birthday party for Jesus where is he?" asked Argent.

"No he's a hermit he won't come!" said Blake who was king of the grim reapers.

"Oh what a shame!" said Argent who was Fate.

there was another knock.

"come in!" Blake shouted again.

in walked another reaper in a Santa suit.

"the soul you wanted to see is here!" said the reaper Morton, Blake's Secretary.

"show him in, dad," said Blake

"come in Tim," said Blake's dad's soul the reaper Morton

in walked a ghost.

"What is going on where is this Halloween town? Jack Skellington is everywhere!" Tim Wong's ghost said.

"this is the afterlife not a cartoon musical!" said Blake

"I heard the skeletons singing!" said Tim

"Argent this is getting crazy!" Blake said exasperated.

"It is Christmas!" Argent said.

"Ok my name is Jack welcome to Halloween town," Blake said exasperatedly.

"Blake!" snapped Argent.

Morton chuckled.

"Who is this ghost?" asked Argent.

"A man whose murder case I am working on!" said Blake

"Murder is not in the spirit of the season Morton send him back to the place he came from." Argent said.

Morton did as he was told.

"but i need to interview him to find his killers!" Blake said.

"no he is not in the spirit of the season!" Argent said.

"but what has his death got to do with anything!" Blake shouted.

"Christmas is love not hate!" Argent said "he died in hate."

"Whatever!" Blake shouted.

Argent heard an off key singer singing a carol he rushed of to chastise them.

leaving Blake arcing blue sparks reading the paperwork to find evidence.

Elsewhere Lance sat in his favourite chair in his home trawling through the paper work as his daughter Kristine watched neighbours on TV loudly.

"Turn it down, Kristine, I'm helping grand dad solve a murder!" shouted Lance who couldn't think and hated the show.

"No I hate hearing Jnr. practising his violin he is terrible!" said Kristine
as in the next room her brother Lance Jnr murdered God Rest Ye Merry Gentlemen.

The next day Blake sat in the morgue at Charring Cross hospital reading the files on the slabs.
Blake was a man not a skeleton now he wore a lab coat glasses and looked like a pen pusher. he sat
on a chair from his office reading.

"Grinch!" said an orderly walking in the room.

"bah humbug!" Blake said frustrated by the interruption.

"We have real work for you!" the orderly said knocking a pile of paperwork off the slab and put a
folder in it's place.

"hey this is police work!" said Blake
the orderly walked off not caring.

"He's so rude!" Blake muttered looking at the mess.

"I'll deal with that later," Blake said picking up the orderly's file and read it and wandered off.
up stairs 5 minutes later.

"Hello you are here for Jack Taylor right?"

"yes who are you?" asked Taylor's wife.

"Dr Alexander, I'm here to tell you how your husband is," Blake said.

"How is he?" asked Mrs Taylor

"He's fine he's waiting for you in his room!" Blake said who was thinking it a prank they usually
sent him to tell people someone died.

When Blake finished his errand of mercy he returned to sort out the mess and continue his work, in
the process he found the name of the person who paid for the hit.

So confident was he they were harmless he went to confront them.

Blake went to their home and was shot and gagged and tied up and was left to die helpless and
wanting to kick himself for not telling anyone where he was.

Blake was missed.

the next day Lance found the name of the hit man.

"Tell me the name of your employer in the Tim Wong hit!" a skeleton in a Santa suit demanded.

"Jack skellington?" the hit man laughed.

"No the necromancer!"" the reaper said. the necromancer was the name Lance was known as the
serial killer.

"Necromancer!" echoed the hit man.

"Tell me his name!" said Lance.
not only did they give a name they gave an address.

"Where is Blake Alexander!" demanded Lance of the person who shot his father.

"Who?" asked the shooter.

"Where is he?" demanded Lance.

"I don't know who he is?" said the shooter.

"You shot him!" Lance said reading the shooters mind.

"What have you done with him!" Lance snapped.
there was a faint knock on a wall.
Lance ran to the wall and found it was a hidden panic room with his near dead father lying within.
he grabbed his father and dematerilized and materialised in Blake's hospital.

he was taken to emergency an they removed the bullet and Lance stayed till he had to leave. weeks later Blake got better. the hit man was arrested, but the shooter escaped the country with someone elses passport and disappeared as if they never existed it was thought they were a spy.

Getting Good Ratings Is Murder

"Our next guest is a multi talented man you may recognise him as Blake Fire, the famous stage magician. He is here as Dr Blake Alexander a coroner and criminologist with the police. His day job." said the host of the Crime Report tv show.

On the stage walked a black haired tall man in a blue suit and glasses.

"Hello Blake welcome to the Crime Report," the host John Taylor said to his guest,

"Hi, John! I watch your show whenever I can. I am glad I could be on it," said Blake

"Nice to hear," John said.

Blake smiled charmingly.

"I would be in trouble with my wife if I didn't talk to you about your magic show," said John.

Blake laughed.

"How do you do your tricks?" asked John half joking.

"David Copperfield would kill me if I revealed the secrets of magic," Blake joked.

John wondered why Blake was wearing glasses as he never wore glasses on the stage as a magician.

Blake pushed up his glasses which weren't falling down.

He was reading John's mind simple telepathy trick nothing hard for a sorcerer like Blake.

"Do you and Max Starfire fight in real life like you do in your show?" John asked.

Blake smiled.

"No not really but he may disagree with me," Blake joked.

They fought like cats and dogs on stage and off but were best of friends.

John laughed.

"I would like to get back to the reason I'm here to discuss the motives of killers," said Blake seriously.

"Yes ok," said John smiling.

"I would be fired if I didn't ask about The Necromancer why does he kill?" asked John.

"He'd kill me If I tell you," Blake said laughing he knew the Necromancer was his son.

"He's is apparently a psychopathic killer who likes to kill," Blake said.

"Yes undoubtedly," John said, "he butchers his victims, he may like the publicity," said John.

"No killers seldom kill for ratings! Although I heard on an ad for 60 minutes a news show on another channel where one apparently did,"

Blake said seriously.

"What happened in case," John asked.

"I don't know I missed the show! I work at night," Blake said.

"Oh! wonder why they did it?" said John.

"To sell his show! Murder can be good for ratings, I suppose," Blake said.

"I suppose so," said John.

Days later a man burst into the dressing room of his co host Henry Jones.

Hours later in the same place.

"Looks like a Necromancer killing." said Sergeant of the local police Simon Xander-Drax.

Blake was examining what was left of the body of Henry Jones.

"No I feel in my bones this is someone else! The man was a saint according to Mortimer." Blake said collecting a tooth from the mess which was all that remained of Henry Jones.

"What are you collecting that tooth for? Are you collecting teeth," asked Max Starfire who was there in a blood red tux and mask.

"No! Sun King I'm collecting it to identify the victim," said Blake.

"I thought you knew who he was Dad," the Necromancer said in a blue tux, top hat and mask.

"Hi Enchanter, they think the Necromancer did this one. I don't thinks so the victim was a sain. The Necromancer's victims are all the worst of the worst why would he change his type of victims?" Blake said.

"That explains why he looks a mess somebody obviously didn't like him." said Lance the Enchanter, "whose the ghoul in the corner of the room."

"Oh him the person who found him," Blake said distracted by something.

"Ok why is he still here?" asked Lance.

"Don't know," Blake said turning to John curiously.

"I am going to do a special on the killing," said John looking slightly green.

"Don't throw up on my crime scene?" snapped Blake a floating bucket materialising under John's head as he threw up.

John's eyes widened he looked shocked.

"How did that happen?" asked John seeing the bucket floating.

"You threw up you can't take the mess!" Blake said.

The bucket dematerialised.

"What the- the bucket where did it come from and go?" asked John having a fit.

"Oh that! I materialised it so you didn't mess up my crime scene!" said Blake frowning down at the shorter man.

"You did! How? you are a stage illusionist!" said John confused.

"May be not just a mere illusionist!" said Max laughing.

"Hey it was just a bucket I didn't bring anyone back from the dead!" said Blake exasperated,

"Not today!" Lance said and chuckled.

Blake glared at his son and turned to John.

"get off my crime scene you will ruin the evidence here!" shouted Blake.

"Ok I'll leave!" said John looking put out by being kicked out of the room.

Days later on the stage on The Crime Report, said John on the show,

"Dr Blake Alexander, Coroner on the case of Henry Jones the old host!"

Blake walked on the stage and sat in a host's chair.

"Hi John," said Blake.

"Hi Dr Alexander," said John.

"Blake is my name nobody calls me Dr Alexander not even the people at my hospital!" Blake said.

"Ok Blake," said John.

"Read the teleprompter!" the director said in their earphones.

Blake cleared his throat.

"Henry was presumed murdered by the serial killer The Necromancer the police are looking for the killer now!" Blake read.

Later at Blake's house.

"Did the Necromancer kill Henry Jones or not?" Blake asked the Necromancer.

"No I was busy killing someone else at the time of the killing you haven't found my victim yet,"

Lance said.

"Then who killed the tv host then?" asked Blake.

"Don't know!" Lance said sighing.

"Must be someone he knew. Most murderers know their victims!" said Blake,

"I'll keep an eye open the killer may do something that may reveal himself."

"Hello Blake how you been," asked John visiting the morgue at Blake's hospital.

"Why are you at the morgue?" said Blake curiously.

"Just visiting my co host what's wrong with that?" asked John.

"We aren't friends!" said Blake said.

"Aw! You hurt me, Blake," said John.

In the room walked an Orderly.

"It's John Taylor! wow you are on The Crime Report every one is talking about the death of your co host," said the Orderly who turned to Blake,

"Hey Dr Death someone died you're needed!" the Orderly pushed a file in Blake's hands and wandered off.

"I hate that guy!" said Blake.

"Dr Death?" said John.

"That's what they call me in this hospital!" said Blake,

"I have to tell someone that someone else died!"

"Why?" asked John.

"Because it's my job!" Blake said.

"Your Job?" said John in disbelief.

"Someone has to tell the families when someone dies!" grumbled Blake.

"Mind if I tag along?" said John.

"Just don't speak to the relatives!" said Blake.

"Ok!" said John.

They wandered off.

"Hello you are here for Kyle Smith," said Blake seeing a group of people who were thinking of a Kyle.

"He's dead," said Blake.

"We know that, he was murdered," said Kyle's wife.

Blake opened the file and look shocked.

"Oh My God! I'm so sorry! He was murdered last Tuesday night by the Necromancer!" Blake said in horror.

"The same time as Henry, oops!" said John thoughtlessly.

Blake turned on him realising the killer was John. Blake's skin paled his eyes grew cold with anger.

"Come with me John!" said Blake grabbing john's wrist near breaking it.

"You're strong!" said John being dragged off into a large medicine room.

"You killed him!" Blake said accusing.

John saw a surgical knife a backed towards it.

"Yes!" said John grabbing it.

"And you cannot live! you must die!" John said coldly as he ran to stab Blake, who dematerialized in his place was a strange creature a skeleton in a black monks outfit. The blade went through the grim reaper.

"Die!" John said.

"You can't kill a reaper!" said the reaper cackling a flaming sword appearing in his hand.

"Necromancer come here I've got the copycat!" said the reaper with Blake's voice.

"You are the grim reaper, Blake?" said John looking nervously at the blade in the Reaper's hand.

"Hello there Dad what we going to do with him?" the black clad masked Necromancer said from behind John as he pointed his sword doom in John's back.

"Throw him to the mortal's law divine justice is not need here!" the reaper said, "Go I will send for the men in blue!"

"Ok," the Necromancer said and the blade in John's back disappeared.

"Simon come I have your killer bring some people with you!" croaked the reaper,

The room was suddenly full of police men.

"Hi Mortimer!" said Simon, " apprehend the human."

"He's Blake Alexander the grim reaper!" shouted John being dragged off.

Simon looked at the reaper and thought that would make sense! For a second both the reaper and Simon looked in each others face. "He'd say anything to get out of trouble," said the reaper.

"You would do the same!" Simon said.

In the room walked Blake.

"Hi Uncle Sie, what you guys doing here? hi Mortimer!" Blake said.

The reaper sighed.

"Hi friend Blake!" said the reaper wondering who was Blake.

In the reaper's head he heard Lance: "I thought he may say something so I came back as you"

Lance heard in his head "Thank you! "

"Maybe I was mistaken," Simon said.

The Grand Reaper

I am Mortimer the grand reaper King of the grim reapers,

I judge the dead and I openly I rule the solar system as It emperor,

I am 2 men in one my soul is called Mortimer, my body is called Blake he's the emperor of the solar system. Blake is an alien sorcerer hero to many. He is many men a coroner and a stage magician, he leads the people of his race.

I has Mortimer rule the lands of the dead and help out the police under the cloak as Blake's friend we share our files and work.

I am father to 2 serial killers who are and were always lead by the nose by fate to do his dirty work as he has no stomach for such violence. One is dead. The other the Necromancer is not. He raised Astra, the daughter of my dead daughter Valkira, the vampire queen Astra is. My other grand daughter the Necromantrix daughter of the Necromancer Is Fate boss she is I am told is Fate's future bride she tells him what to do.

We are complicated people.

Yes Fate is real he's a man. He's a ham actor. Argent Lumiere the Fate is the last of his race of fate well he was till my wife came to be. She is one too. She exist because my first wife was murdered. She was reincarnated as my now second wife.

Bit weird and confusing being married to your ex-wife never know what we experienced in this life and the last.

Bad Omens or the insane unfortunate ravings of a mad chicken

The day began like most others. Blake Alexander yawned as he got ready for work at Charing Cross hospital. Where he was the coroner in charge of the morgue.

His wife was on holiday without him in America so it would be lonely at work.

He heard the doorbell and dashed to answer the door.

He found at it a slightly nervous man a Postman.

"Hello," Blake said wondering why he was nervous.

"Here is a letter for you sir," said the postman, "please don't take my life yet I have some paperwork to do. It's my will."

Blake laughed.

"You're alright man I don't take the living," said Blake.

"I need a signature for the letter," the postman said.

Blake signed for the letter and took it inside to read.

To Blake's surprise it wasn't addressed to him.

"It must be a prank!" He thought.

His mobile phone rang and still, he thought nothing odd was happening,

He answered it.

"That's the best joke yet was it you who thought it up,"

said Lance his son laughing down the line.

"What? " Blake asked.

"Sending a letter to me via registered post addressed to the antichrist, " Lance laughed.

"Strange I got one to Death," said Blake, "I thought it was a work prankster! "

Blake opened the envelope

"What does your letter say?" Asked Blake.

"TO THE ANTICHRIST,

COME TO ARMAGEDDON NEEDED TO END THE WORLDS" Lance said.

"Mine is the same except for it asks death to go there, Lance, this is suspicious," said Blake.

A moment later something decidedly odd happened. Out of thin air appeared a man in the closed house.

"Blake hi I tried to call you but you were on the phone," the man said.

"Max! hi, something weird is going on apparently! Lance is the antichrist and I am Death!" Blake Laughed, "No truth stretched there. I'm the King of the grim reapers and that is practically Death anyway. But, him the antichrist really!" Blake said, "He's mad but not evil!"

"Well at least you weren't called pestilence or a harlot!" said Max shortly.

"What!" snapped Blake shocked.

"Astra is very upset they called her a harlot!" said Max.

"and you were called pestilence and were told to go to Armageddon," Blake said.

"yes, wonder who else got letters," said Max.

"Who knows could be anyone who sent it to anyone they don't like much," Blake said.

"Any idea where they want us to go?" asked Max.

"The Mount of Megiddo," Blake said.

"What? Where is that?" Max said.

"The middle east near Israel!" Said Lance materializing.

"Hey I'm not going there they won't let us come home for years!" said Max.

"Who says! I went there last week!" Lance said.

"Just the Australian Politicians they want to ban people going there and coming back soon as they leave!" said Max.

"It's to stop people who want to go on holy war!" said Blake.

"Why did they let you back in the country!" Max asked.

"He was on reaper business," said Blake,

"We aren't going anywhere!"

"Then what are we going to do then?" Lance asked.

"Not sure!" Blake said sadly.

Max's phone rang. He answered it.

"Astra hi! now slow down! What! you said what!"

Alexa turn on tv!" Max said. Blake's tv turned on and a voice chirped back "Ok!"

"Look! Astra told me to turn on the tv!" said Max.

"Yes aliens are out there, and they are at the Whitehouse pledging friendship. The president greeted their leader," said the tv. On the tv was President Trump shaking hands with a grey x-zerracian alien.

"I can't believe it!" Max said.

"I welcome our interstellar neighbours to our world and welcome them in friendship!" the president said.

"And people think he's the antichrist!" said Lance.

"They said they would never reveal themselves to the world this isn't right!" Blake said.

"what about the ones who asked you to take them to your leader!" said Lance.

"It was nothing official! but this is!" Blake said.

"Why am I here? I was told to come here where is the emperor of this system who is this human!" the leader of the greys said in their language on the tv.

Max, Blake and Lance laughed. They spoke x-zerracian fluently Blake was the Emperor the grey spoke of.

"It is thought this is a greeting to the president!" the tv said.

"It's an insider!" said Blake.

"How do you know!" asked Max.

"Only we knew of them and us!" said Blake,

"I'll see a man who knows everything"

"Alexa read Good Omens" a man sitting in a chair in front of a glowing pond of water holding a Kindle Fire device said.

"Aziraphale looked down at his feet, and swore for the second time in five minutes." read the kindle device.

"That needs a charger!" Blake said appearing.

"What do I need a charger for?" the man said.

"oh fuck," the device said moments later and the battery died.

Although such language was abhorrent to the 2 men, they did see a certain amount of irony in such last words. Blake feeling sorry for the man his other son Tempus. Blake said "Abracadabra! It's charged," like a conjurer, Blake zapped the device and it blew up.

"Oops, wrong voltage", Blake said.

"Dad!! Now I won't find out what happened," Tempus said

"How did that work," asked Blake.

"Don't know I bought it off eBay. Now I won't know if Armageddon happened or not."

"I am here to stop it happening" Blake added,

"What do you mean stop Armageddon," Tempus asked.

"Just that the dead are rising. Apparently, Max, Lance Astra and I have something to do with it, we got letters calling us to the middle east. Oh and the x-zerracians want to be friends with Trump! They also wonder who he is.

My letter was addressed to Death. Lance was amused by his, he's supposed to be the antichrist. Max is pestilence. Astra was insulted hers was addressed to the harlot. We don't know who sent them to us," Blake explained. The gate of the underworld had been stuck open since he saw the aliens on tv.

This was the man who'd know what was its genesis. Not because he was omnipresent. He wasn't it was because of the pool of water which showed events in time.

"Oh, I see now!" Tempus said and readied the pool of time for the job.

"I see it now look," said Tempus pointing at the pool.

"What is the Masked Chicken doing with that! It is the book of fate it has the power to change reality," Blake said, "how did he get it!"

"I'll look!" said Tempus.

They saw him walking in a park and seeing and picking up the book. In his hand was an open book Good Omens by Terry Pratchett and Neil Gaiman.

"I'm reading that too," said Tempus.

"I see he is writing his version of it in real life!" said Blake.

"He may not know he is bringing on the end of time," said Tempus.

"To fix it you need to send me back to the time he finds it," said Blake.

"Alright!" said Tempus the Timekeeper lord of time, "That door will take you to him."

Blake walk through the door and appeared out of a portal there.

"Hello Blake how are you doing?" said the masked chicken.

"Give me that you idiot it is not your book!" Blake snapped grabbing the book from the chicken with an almost rude attitude.

"Hey what's with the attitude, my friend," asked the chicken shocked.

"You started the apocalypse! and Astra is no harlot! This is the Enchantress's book, not yours!" said Blake, "go read your book if you want an apocalypse!" added Blake walking back into the portal. "What a strange man!" said the Chicken.

next thing Blake saw was the halls of time and Tempus sitting in his chair.

"Take the next door to see the Enchantress," Tempus said.

"Ok," Blake said and took it.

He saw a teenage girl who was crying in a library alone.

She was Lance's daughter the Enchantress Kristine.

"Hey now Krissy the Apocalypse is over here's your book!" said Blake to his granddaughter giving her the book she had lost. She hugged him.

"Thanks, granddad I was really worried it would fall in the wrong hands, I lost it!" Kristine said.

"Be more careful it's a powerful book. It fell into bad hands but it's back now where it belongs," Blake said.

Flashpoint

"Why did you abduct me?" the coroner of police asked nervously of his abductor. "You desecrated my wife's body," said the abductor. "Oh, you are mad! I autopsied her, I'm the coroner, "No it was a desecration," said the abductor. "You don't know who I am I observe," said the coroner frowning. "I know who you are you are the man who tore apart my wife!" the abductor. "I see you are not going to see the truth!" said the coroner wondering how on Earth the mad man was overpowering him a sorcerer. "Uncle Sie I need the police," Blake, the coroner cried. "Who's your uncle and how do expect him to hear you?" asked the abductor. "You'll find out!" said Blake darkly. "Midnight what do you want?" said a police sergeant surrounded by the bewildered policeman. Who all appeared out of thin air. The abductor runs to the coroner placing a knife to the coroner's neck drawing a little blood. To the shock of the abductor It was not human blood it was blue static energy. "what are you?" asked the abductor asked in horror. "Not human obviously," said the shocked coroner. "Let him go!" ordered the sergeant. The abductor could not resist doing want the sergeant said. He was under the spell of a powerful enchanter. "and drop that knife!" said the sergeant. Abductor released Blake dropped and the knife. Standing hypnotized standing like a stunned fish was the abductor. "Are you alright Midnight?" asked Sergeant Simon Xander-Drax of his grand nephew. As other policemen untied him from the chair he was tied to. "I may need a band-aid! but I'm alright! Thank you for coming quickly!" Blake said then a band-aid appeared over his wound stopping the flow of blood coming from his neck. "He abducted me fro the hospital," Blake said. "Mr. Morcroft why did you abduct my Nephew? asked the Sergeant. "To kill him he desecrated my wife's corpse!" said the abductor in a daze. "He's a nutter!" said Blake, "I autopsied her he calls it desecration.". "Obviously he's a nutter, take away Mr. Morcroft for processing." the sergeant said. "I have to go I have some paperwork to do!" Blake said and disappeared in thin air. "But I have to know what happened!" Simon said, "I'll talk to you later then!"

The Writing is on the Wall

"Strange graffiti!" said a tall pale man in a blood-red tux and top hat wearing a mask.
"It's not graffiti! It's a blood splatter but don't get excited," the coroner. He a tall black-haired man in a lab coat and glasses said matter of factly to the vampire king.
"Why would he get excited by blood?" the police sergeant the great uncle of the coroner. he looked like his grandnephew and the vampire surprisingly young about 25. Obviously, there was something strange about them. What it was they weren't human they were alien sorcerors who stopped aging at 25. The sergeant didn't know the vampire was a vampire.
"I wouldn't know," said Max the vampire glaring at the coroner.
"What happen another murder of the Necromancer?" asked the Sergeant.
"No a reaper took the dead woman," said the coroner flatly.
"How do you know,' asked the sergeant.
"I was told I asked the king of the reapers, Mortimer who killed them," the Coroner said as if it was something normal.
"Oh why the stain on the wall?" asked Max.

Earlier in the same place

The Reaper knew the victim but she didn't know him he had been so anxious to meet her there was a problem. He was scared of her recognizing him he acted aloof but his heart was racing.
"Vivienne you will die there are no buts about it," a skeletal man in Benedictine monks outfit said. said Vivienne in reply "but-but-" staring at his head.

The Reaper huffed "Stop saying but! you can't deny or bargain with me!" Vivienne took a deep breath and said: "So you came for me?"

Death said as sharply as a blade " yes! I have! You died at midnight" Vivienne sobbed slightly and said "Midnight? It is 5 to midnight!"

The Reaper looked as awkward as a skeleton could. Vivienne cried triumphantly as a prisoner reprieved execution would "You're early! I live!" The Reaper understood.

The Reaper said nervously "I will take you at midnight!" Vivienne asked nearly as nervously as the reaper was "what killed me tonight?"

The Reaper snapped back "I did!" Vivienne shook her head saying "not you! my cause of death can you tell me or is it forbidden,"

Death laughed and said " stroke! It started when you awoke!"

Vivienne shouted "I am not having a stroke! I am not dying" the Reaper said, "Then why are you crying?"

the Reaper said, "and why are you speaking like you are having a stroke, my dear?" Vivienne noticed she was having a stroke she recognizes the symptoms she was struck by fear!

her death was coming and coming soon, five minutes had passed she died alone with Death in the light of the moon.

"Why did he choose me to take you! He knows I know you!"
the reaper hit the wall of the room in frustration. Blood streaked across the wall he left with Vivienne's soul.
Later...
"It was the Necromancer in reaper form. Apparently, the girl was an old flame of his he was angry he had to take her he hit the wall in frustration. it was nothing sinister." said Dr. Alexander who was known as Dr. Death at the hospital he worked. He was the father of the reaper who left the mark otherwise known as Mortimer.

No Turning Back

"We have your wife and daughter," a man said over the phone to magician Max Starfire. Who sat alone in his dark dressing room in his theatre.

"Max! why so serious?" said Blake Fire doing a Joker impression seeing his worried face as he walked in the room. Blake was his partner in the magic act.

"Shut up, Blake this is serious! Go away!" Max snapped back,

"We can use him too," the voice on the phone said, "tell him to stay we will use him too,".

"Blake please don't go! They need you!" Max said.

"Who needs me?" asked Blake.

"The people who say they have Astra and little Astry," Max burst out.

"Have they any proof they have them?" asked Blake.

"Nothing but their word so far," said Max,

"Put it on speaker phone I'll close the door," Blake said.

Max turned on speaker phone and Blake closed the door.

"Do you have proof you have them?" Blake said.

"You want proof it is only natural! talk to them, girl," the voice on the phone ordered.

a child spoke: "Daddy what is going on?" Max looked peaked.

Blake's blood drained from his face and he paled.

"Daddy will save you Astry," said Max.

"Is that enough proof?" the voice on the phone said.

"What do you want?" Max said into the phone.

"For you 2 to rob the NAB bank in Croydon," said the voice on the phone.

"You want us to what?" asked Blake thinking it was a joke.

"I told you! the voice said.

"Why?" Max asked.

"There are some papers in the vault we need!" the voice said.

"We can't rob a bank!" Blake said, "who do you think we are?"

"Very desperate men who will do anything to save the ones you love!"

the voice said.

"Why pick on us?" Blake asked.

"You are experts with security and locks and Max is the protegé of the greatest thieves of the era!" said the voice.

"Finally someone respects me! And for something other than being a banshee reporting when people die in the hospital!" Blake said.

"Dr. Death, shut up!" said Max.

"What is he talking about!" asked the voice on the phone.

"At his work they use him to tell people when someone dies in his hospital," Max said.

"Why would they use a magician to tell people when someone dies? does he raise them from the dead?" chuckled the voice on the phone.

"Now that's silly nobody rises from the dead, Hey! Max," Blake who was amused by the joke said.

"He's an expert when it comes to death his day job as coroner," said Max.

"He's a coroner?" asked the voice.

"Yes," Blake said.

"What do you want us to take?" asked Max.

"Don't tell the police!" asked the voice.

"We won't," Blake promised.

"Meet me in the car park near the bank at midnight in masks so nobody knows you!" the voice said and the call ended.

Later that night.

"This is ripe! We are in masks trying to rob a bank" Blake said in an ironical tone. "We'll be recognized." They were noted masked superheroes. So anyone would say why are Blue Midnight (Blake) and The Sun King (Max) robbing a bank.

"Stoop a little look shorter," Max who wore a white satin mask said as both were tall.

"Where is the guy on the phone?" Blake asked.

They heard the humming of a drone coming from the sky.

"Why do you look so familiar," asked the voice from the phone coming from the drone.

"We are famous!" said Blake.

"Yes must be it!" said the voice.

They walked to the front of the bank.

Max pulled out a gadget.

"what's that?" the drone asked.

"It's a toy!" Max said activating it.

The cameras turned off. He pressed a few more buttons

the alarm went off and the bank's automatic door opened.

"Come on!" said Max walking in the bank.

they walked through the bank Max pressing buttons and doors opened. They got to the vault.

"What are you doing here?" a young guard said staring at them perplexed.

"he has a gun!" said Max.

"Of course I have a gun I'm a guard! Hey how did you even get in here!" said the guard pointing his gun at them.

"Magic," said Max laughing he tried to put his toy! in his pocket the movement made the guard shoot. Max fell to the ground.

"Hey, we aren't armed!" Blake said kneeling to see if his friend was alright.

"Oh?" said the guard worried, "is your friend alright?"

"He was shot in the heart what do you think!" snapped Blake.

"Don't bite my head off," the guard said dropping his gun in shock and Blake grabbed it.

"Don't tempt me, boy," Blake told the guard who looked nervous seeing a gun in Blake's hand trained on him.

"We should lock the guard in the vault when we go!" the drone said.

"Come with us lead the way," ordered Blake waving the gun.

"What will we do with your friend?" the drone asked.

"Leave him he's dead!" Blake said, " what you want me to do give the gun to the boy and me carry my dead friend?"

"No bad Idea!" said the drone.

They went into the vault.

The drone fell to the ground and screams emitted from it.

"sounds like the vampire king has saved his family, I'd hate to be the one who took his family," said the guard.

"Yes son," Blake told Lance his son who was posing as a guard.

"Why did Daddy attack them Mummy?" the drone said,

"He saved us,"

"Get out of there you two do you want to be caught?" asked Max through the drone.

"Yes!" said Blake looking at the drone turning his head.

The drone exploded in blue sparks into nothingness.

"Why'd you explode it?" asked Lance.

"Getting rid of the evidence," Blake said.

"Let's go!" Lance said hearing people coming.

They disappeared into thin air.

In ran a perplexed witness to the empty scene of the crime

Out of Time

"It's dark tonight I hope we aren't seen," a man said to his partner in crime.

"It's like the old days we climb in a window and pray not to get caught," said the thief who was known as the Chameleon to his partner the Cat as they stealthily walked through the garden of their mark.

"The room is the third window on the second story," said the Cat examining the building. The Chameleon tested the strength of a lattice leading to it going up the wall.

"This should work I'm surprised people are so careless with security," the Chameleon said laughing.

They climbed up the lattice trying not to be pricked by the thorns of the rose that climbed up it also.

"The alarm is off or it should be, but I'll disable it," said the Chameleon.

He cut the alarm wire and jimmied the window till it opened.

They climbed in the room and looked about it.

"The safe is behind that painting," said the Chameleon pointing at the only picture in the room.

"Ok who will do the work you or me?" asked the Cat who was as skilled a cracksman as the Chameleon.

"It's my turn you did the last job," said the Chameleon who walked over to the picture removing it handing it to the Cat to put down. The Chameleon put his ear to the safe and cracked the lock and opened the door removing the contents out of the safe putting it in a backpack on the Cat's back.

"Got it! Let's go." said the Chameleon.

The next day the police were swarming around the house.

"Midnight, what happened here?" the police sergeant asked.

"A robbery," said Blake, the coroner who helped out the police on other cases.

"I know, Midnight," said sergeant Xander-Drax frowning, "do we have any idea how it was done and ideas who they were or why they were here?"

"They were copycats," said Blake who was otherwise known as the superhero Blue Midnight.

"Copycats?" said the Sergeant "of who?".

"The Cat and The Chameleon," Blake said.

"What they must be old," said the sergeant.

"Not old dead," Blake said.," that's why I say, copycats!"

"How do you know they were copycats?" the sergeant asked.

The CCTV caught the robbery they were young men in their twenties," one was dressed as the cat burglar, the Cat. His partner was dressed as the Chameleon the jewel thief and safecracker," said Blake. " My Magician's assistant Max is the original Chameleon's grandson and protege. He should be on the case."

"Yes," said the sergeant.

"I'll call him here," said Blake, who then shouted, "Max we need you."

Out of thin air appeared a dishevelled man holding a toothbrush in his PJs.

"What do you want Blake," asked the man.

"Get dressed Max, you are a mess!" Blake said to the man.

"Right," said Max who waved his arm and appeared well groomed in a suit. Blake looked at him oddly " What Blake!" Max asked.

"Toothbrush!" Blake said. Max saw he was still holding his toothbrush it disappeared.

"Why did you call me here I was brushing my teeth," Max said.

"We need your help on a case," said the Sergeant.

."What sort of case? Murder?" asked Max.

"No robbery this place was robbed by a ghost from the past. Actually your past," said Blake.

"What?" said Max.

"The Cat and the Chameleon," said Blake.

"Can't be Granddad is dead and so is Uncle Mike," said Max.

"I know!" Blake said.

"Someone dressed up as them to rob this place," said the sergeant.

"Why would they get copycats," asked Max.

"We don't know," said Blake.

"What did they take?" asked Max.

"Money, Jewelry and Papers," Blake said.

"What papers?" asked Max.

"Business papers," said the owner of the house was standing with them.

"What were they?" asked Max.

"Mostly IOUs! I'm a money lender," the owner said. Max looked at him and felt a sudden disgust. The owner of the house looked like a pen pusher.

"Judging already," Blake said in Max's mind.

"Sorry," Max said in Blake's mind.

"From what I've read he is more of a bureaucrat than you take me for," Blake said in Max's mind.

"Are granddad and Uncle Mike still in the other world," asked Max in Blake's mind.

"Yes," said Blake also known as Mortimer, king of the grim reapers in Max's mind.

"You two talking in telepathy again?" asked the sergeant.

"Oh I forgot you were there Uncle Sie," said Blake to the sergeant.

"Did someone see them," asked Max.

Blake showed him a video on his work tablet.

"What is it Max?" asked Blake seeing his friend's eyes widen.

"I know them!" said Max.

"Who are they?" asked Blake.

"Michel and Maximilien Black!" said Max.

"What the-" the Sergeant said.

"Are they related to you?" Blake asked.

"Yes," Max said, "But they shouldn't be here!"

"What do you mean," asked Blake.

"I saw photos of Grandad and Uncle Mike in the past that is them down to the voices," said Max.

"I just figured out this case!" snapped Blake frowning,

A dimension away a man was watching them in a magic pond. He gulped and said "oh no!" He was watching them.

"Tempus have you been messing with history again?" Blake said in the pond.

Tempus stepped out of a dark swirling vortex in the room with Blake and the others nervously.

"Whose he is he your brother?" asked the house's owner because there was a family resemblance between Tempus and Blake.

"No my meddling son the lord of time, the Timekeeper, Tempus.

The man behind this crime!" said Blake.

"I see what he did Blake!" said Max realizing what happened.

"What did he do?" asked the homeowner.

"He took the young thieves from the past to rob you," said Blake.

"What? That is impossible!" laughed the homeowner thinking it was a joke.

"Not for him he lives in the tunnels of time," said Blake.

"I want to meet them!" said Max pleading

"You'll meet them later," said Tempus.

"How? Not in the afterlife! I'll not go there you know I'm a vampire," said Max.

"Spoilers!" said Tempus.

"Why did you bring them here and turn off the alarm?" Blake asked.

"I wanted to stop a blackmailer," said Tempus.

"A what?" asked the sergeant looking at the homeowner who was trying to look calm.

"Who was being blackmailed and how?" asked Blake.

"Mr. Harvey's debtors," said Tempus said.

"How?" asked Max

"I cannot go there as it will ruin the lives of many people!" said Tempus.

"Why they were only IOUs," the sergeant said.

"Not all of them he had people watched and got dirt on his clients to extort more money from them," said Tempus.

"Where are the papers and things taken?" asked Blake.

"Maxim and Michael fenced the things in the past." said Tempus, "the papers I burned there are somethings nobody should know."

"We have no evidence!" said the sergeant.

"You have me!" said Tempus.

"Are you giving in to the police," said Blake.

"No! I was a victim!" said Tempus

"You took out a loan from him?" Max asked.

"No he was blackmailing me!" said Tempus.

"Why?" said the sergeant.

"I killed a man, Mum's killer. He found out and has been blackmailing me since he found out!" said Tempus.

"What did he want from you?" asked Blake.

"For me to get dirt on people!" said Tempus.

"To blackmail people," Blake said.

Tempus nodded.

"I had to get back and destroy the letters I sent him," said Tempus, "so I enlisted some friends from the past to take them for me"

The homeowner was thinking he shouldn't have reported the theft.

"You are probably right mate," said Blake aloud after reading his mind.

"Arrest him!" said the sergeant.

A policeman grabbed Tempus who looked sorry for what he'd done and didn't fight.

"Not him he's the victim!" said the sergeant, "arrest Mr. Harvey! He's the criminal!"

The policeman released Tempus and the handcuffs on Tempus's wrists fell off.

"What the-" the policeman said he picked up the cuffs and unlocked them to put them on, Mr. Harvey.

"He admitted to murder and you arrest me why?" said Mr. Harvey.

"I know the story! He did it to save a life!" said the sergeant who looked at Blake knowingly.

Blake looked confused.

"I know who you are Mortimer!" said the sergeant in Blake's mind.

"Mortimer?" Blake said aloud looking like a stunned fish recovering he dematerialized.

"Who is Mortimer?" said Mr. Harvey hearing Blake.

"You'll meet him later," said Tempus.

The sergeant and Max laughed.

"Who's he?" asked Mr. Harvey being lead away.

"He's scared and confused," the sergeant said.

Beyond Believing

Blake Alexander stood peering out through a crack in a curtain at his son's house. He looked as nervous as he was.

"Why is super dork hiding in our house dork?" asked Blake's teenage grandson of his father Lance who he called dork.

"The men in black are chasing him," Lance said.

"Yeah right dork!" said Lance Jnr who didn't believe he was of an alien race let alone they were sorcerers and the fact the men in black were real was just ridiculous.

"He's meant to be the emperor of the solar system why doesn't he tell them to go away!" said Kristine, Lance's daughter sarcastically.

"I tried they don't recognize the empire," said Blake who was distracted,

"they're coming to the door where can I hide?"

There was a distant voice behind them.

"Dad hide here!" the voice said it was not Lance's voice but his other son's voice it emitted from a whirling dark vortex.

Blake jumped in it and it disappeared.

There was a knock at the front door.

"Children don't follow me there could be some danger at the door," said Lance the children followed him in spite of him.

"go away!" snapped Lance rolling his eyes.

"No they are just hawkers not men in anything!" said Kristine.

"I'll protect you even If you don't deserve it!" Lance said frustratedly.

He opened the door.

"That's not Will Smith I wanted to meet him!" jnr said.

One of the men in black rolled his eyes.

"why do people always say that? Do I look like an actor? Is this a movie?" he snapped frustratedly.

"Excuse my colleague he is a little ill-tempered," the other man in black said apologetically.

"I understand his frustration," said Lance, "What do you want?"

"You are the son of Blake Alexander?" said the apologetic man in black.

"I am, what does that matter? has he made a mistake in his paperwork?" asked Lance calmly.

"We are looking for him," replied the 2nd man,

"Why?" asked Lance.

"He is a suspect in a case," the 1st man said.

"What case?" said Lance.

The 2nd man glared at his friend for mentioning their case.

"A case of -" said the 1st.

"You look for him because he met aliens!" Lance said straightly.

"You know who we are?" said the 1st man confused.

"I can read minds!" said Lance smiling.

"Yeah right dork!" said Kristine.

"Not now, girl," said Lance releasing the venom that was thinly veiled below his calm attitude.

The men in black wondered what man they really met.

"Why are you scared I don't bite!" laughed Lance who read their minds.

"He doesn't bite! He kills with a sword," said jnr.

"he does what?" said man 1 in horror.

"Jnr! shut up!" said Lance turning to his son, "I kill no one,"

Lance fate's assassin lied.

"Go away My father is not here, I don't like him why would I hide him!" screamed Lance slamming the door in the faces of the men in black.

"What was that?" said the 1st man not sure what just happened.

"That man is dangerous we should avoid him I fear we might end up dead if we don't he has the aura of a killer," the 2nd man said running off to their car.

Elsewhere a dimension away sitting by a magic pool Blake sat laughing.

"They don't know how right he was the Necromancer was only a hairs breath from killing them!" Blake who read his son's mind as he watched them in the scrying pond in the tunnels of time where his other son Tempus lived.

"I would not go back for a while if I were you, he's too angry we can't have him killing you instead he really hates you!" Tempus said.

"Yes It would be awkward doing the paperwork!" said Blake imagining him the secret king of the grim reapers interviewing himself to find out how he died and judging his sins to tell if he went to heaven or hell.

The Alien Invasion

"What is that a plane crashing in the park? I better investigate," thought Blake Alexander seeing a strange light in the sky.

It turned out to be a UFO landing.

"Oh an x-zeracian ship," said Blake recognizing it.

"Should be neighborly and see what they want. "

"Take us to your leader," the grey alien said,

"I am my leader, the emperor of this system," said Blake, "what brings you to my system."

"We want to make our presence known," the alien said.

"You are known I've seen you're people before I'm descended from your race," Blake said.

"Oh," said the alien, " then we'll go."

Then they left again. Sad and dejected they wanted to make the first contact and they met one of the descendants of their race so they weren't first.

It wasn't the end of this Blake was chased for months later by the men in black till they realized he was not going to be a problem as he was an alien like the men in black and the x-zerracians so it was merely an alien meeting aliens.

"I saw the leader of the hybrid aliens the one who calls himself the Emperor of the solar system! I saw him meeting aliens at a ufo. They were trying to invade, he must have told them to leave because he was the ruler!" said Professor Charles Potts.

"You heard what they said?" asked Lance Alexander.

"No saw them they spoke to him and left!" said Potts.

"How do you know what they said then?" Lance asked

"He is an alien autocrat," said Potts.

"No he is a diplomat! He must have asked them for paperwork they didn't have that would be the only reason they would leave so fast!" said Lance, who knew his father Blake, he saw him as obsessed with paperwork, as he was always moaning about it.

"Like that would happen think boy," Potts said the apparently younger man who was twice his age and only looked younger because of his races habit of aging to 25 and stopping growing older.

"But Professor-" said Lance.

"We must stop this alien invasion!" said Potts.

"Alien invasion what alien invasion!" said Lance laughing.

"We must exterminate their king?" said Potts.

"Exterminate their king? what do you think they are a cockroach infestation?" asked Lance.

"Worse I wouldn't wear this hat if they were cockroaches!" said Potts pointing at a leather hat on his head with a plastic lining poking out.

"I wanted to ask you about that," laughed Lance.

"It is lined with velostat!" Potts said.

"Isn't that packing stuff?" said Lance.

"Yes but it is an electrically conductive polymeric foil," said Potts.

"Did you make it yourself?" asked Lance.

"No I bought it from a guy in America he makes them why?" asked Potts.

"Why are you wearing a foil hat!" asked Lance.

"No one can mess with my mind when I wear it!" said Potts.

"I'm sorry somebody has already messed with your mind if you think Blue Midnight is the leader of an alien invasion he's too straight-laced to start an invasion!" said Lance.

"He as hypnotized you too!" said Potts to his friend.

"I rather doubt that!" said Lance, "Sorry but you'd see Superman and say he is the vanguard of an alien invasion."

"He is!" said Potts.

"Blue Midnight is a superhero, not a danger! He'd bore you to death with his repeated references to paperwork," said Lance, " the only operations he performs are autopsies, he's a coroner."

"Are you defending him," asked Potts.

"Me? I want you to see the truth! He is no danger!" said Lance.

"He is the leader of a hive of alien hybrids who have taken over the world in secret!" said Potts.

"Great now he's the leader of the Illuminati!" Lance said.

"No an alien invasion!" said Potts.

Later.

"A friend of mine wants to kill you dad for being the leader of an alien invasion," Lance said to Blake at his father's office in the underworld.

"What?" said Blake shocked.

"You are the leader of a hybrid alien race and you need to be stopped," Lance said.

"Come off it boy," Blake said, "What is his danger level Dark Sorceror very imminent danger or Masked Chicken a danger to only him?" "Actually he's Masked Chicken Level!" said Lance sadly.

"You protect him for me," Blake said.

"Alright," said Lance.

"I won't let him hurt anyone else," said Blake.

"Else?" asked Lance.

"He killed an alien hybrid or thinks he did they were actually a regular human, a dentist no loss there," said Blake who disliked dentists.

"He murdered a dentist," Lance said.

"Yes here is his death certificate," said Blake a paper apparated in his hand and he gave it to his son.

"I see," said Lance bursting with joy.

"Are you alright boy?" asked Blake

"I have a plan," said Lance.

"This is Blake's show," said Lance to Potts at the magic show of Blake and his assistant Max.

"I know," said Potts.

"We can get him here when he is distracted," Lance said.

"Ok," said Potts.

"I need an assistant from the audience," said Blake on the stage.

"Here's your chance," Lance said.

Potts volunteered.

"This is a dangerous trick it has killed many magicians," said Blake handing a gun to Potts after proving it real

"Fire it at me I will catch the bullet in my teeth," Blake said.

"Die you alien monster!" cried Potts firing at Blake's heart.

The bullet went through Blake as it would a ghost.

Max grabbed Potts and he turned into Blake on stage walked Max, the real Max.

"How did you do this?" asked Potts.

"With magic and a little help from my friends," Blake said

Lance walked on to the stage.

With a Policeman.

"He murdered Gary Barlow because he thought he was an alien," said Lance coldly.

"My friend?" said Potts pitifully.

"My son," said Blake.

"and he attempted to murder Blake Alexander," Lance said.

Lance gave the policeman some paperwork, including the death certificate and the ghost of Mr Barlow's interview given by the king of the grim reaper's Blake himself.

"Come with me Potts!" said Sergeant Simon Xander- Drax, Blake's great uncle.

"Professor Potts to you," Potts shouted.

"Okay, Professor Potts? Why do you hate aliens so much we're harmless," Simon said dragging Potts off.

The audience's applause rang through the theatre.

Blake bowed to the audience.

Whispers from Pandemonium or Once In a Blue Midnight

Whispers from Pandemonium or Once In a Blue Midnight

There were whispers that the reaper king Mortimer once lost his human form, his body, his shell. Among the reapers, rumors changed it to his soul being stolen.

This is what really happened,

Blake Alexander bowed to his audience from his stage so did his partner in his magic act Max Starfire. They dematerialized and rematerialized in their dressing room backstage.

"Max you never do things right in the act why do you try to pull a hat from a rabbit you know it never works!" Blake said, "I was covered in blood I had to change!"

"I am trying to get it to work!" Max said sadly thinking of the dead rabbit.

"trust a vampire you just wanted to see blood again!" Blake snapped,

"I did not, I'm not a mad ghoul like Renfield! I only drink human blood! Animal blood is as disturbing to me as it is to you!" Max retorted.

They did not speak for the rest of the night. Blake being brooding over the innocent lives lost. Max brooding over the accusation that he liked to kill rabbits.

The next day the local coroner was autopsying a murder victim when this happened.

A male orderly burst into the room.

"You! Oh what do you want?" the coroner said seeing him.

"We have a job for you! We have another freshy for you!" said the orderly dropping a folder "I'm busy now!" snapped the doctor.

"It's your only job here!" said the orderly curtly.

"Oh alright John Doe can wait if he must!" said the doctor,

"You won't stop until I do what you want." the doctor dropped his surgical knife and removed his bloody gloves and changed lab coats. As he was stained with blood on the sleeve.

He picked up the folder and began to read.

"Take me to them," he said as he read.

The orderly lead him to a room with a dead man in.

"Myocardial infarction!" said the orderly "Ok go do your work." the orderly led the doctor to a group of worried people.

"This is Dr. Death he wants to speak to you about the patient!" the orderly said and walked off.

"Dr. Death what an odd name!" the wife of the dead man said.

"That's not my name I'm actually called Dr. Blake Alexander but for some reason, they call me Dr. Death! I am a coroner!" said the Doctor.

"Coroner? What does this mean?" asked the wife.

"I'm afraid it is what you think it means!" said Blake reading her mind.

"He's dead!" the wife said bursting into tears on the doctor's shoulder.

"How?" asked the dead man's brother.

"he had a myocardial infarction!" said Blake as he tried to comfort the wife.

"A what?" the wife of the brother said.

"Myocardial infarction is doctor speak for a heart attack!" Blake said.

The wife sobbed more.

Max materialized nearby seeing Blake embracing the wife.

"I'll tell Angela I saw you in the arms of another woman!" Max laughed.

"Oh! Shut up you demented vampire this woman just lost her husband, I'm comforting her!" Blake snapped "What do you want?"

"I need to borrow you!" said Max.

"Borrow me?" Blake said, "How?"

Later, at a crime scene nearby.

"Blue Midnight what do you think killed her?" a masked man in a red magician's outfit asked another a masked man. His friend wore a blue magician's outfit he was squatting over the victim's wound sniffing.

"Are you an idiot! She was shot!" Blake who was the blue masked man said, his eyes darkening behind the mask, "can't you see the bullet hole. I don't have to be a coroner to tell you that!"

"Blake I'm not an idiot I can see the hole! I asked because you talk to the dead I thought you may have talked to her spirit," Max the man in red said.

"I may be a necromancer, but I can't talk to a spirit that is not there!" Blake said frowning.

"You mean a reaper took her for processing anyone we know?" Max asked in Blake's head.

"Yes, as a matter of fact, it was another necromancer, I smelt his magic on her," Blake said in Max's head.

"You don't mean it was him?" Max replied in Blake's head.

"Yes, the Necromancer! He does reaper duties too," Blake said telepathically to Max.

"Good we have a witness!" said Max thoughtlessly out loud.

"Oh good, who?" asked the police sergeant walking up to them.

Max panicked he was the last person he wanted to know the Necromancer was the witness! He was the man who raised his wife she'd kill him if he did anything to hurt her uncle the Necromancer!

"A reaper!" said Max.

"Mortimer?" asked the Sergeant.

"Hmm? What-?" muttered Blake forgetting who he was then in truth he was Mortimer king of the grim reapers.

"Blake are you alright?" asked the sergeant. "Hmm? Me? I'm fine, Uncle Simon," Blake said

"I thought we lost you for a minute!" Simon Xander-Drax his great-uncle said laughing.

"Me too for a second!" said Blake.

Simon looked worried.

Max was hoping he would forget the witness.

"If not friend Mortimer then who?" asked Simon.

"I'll organize an interview," Blake said.

"How do we get the help of Mortimer?" asked Simon who didn't know Blake's secret.

"I'll deal with it," Blake said.

"You want me to what?" the Necromancer said choking on a cup of coffee later.

"Go to the police station in reaper form and tell them what you saw in Jenifer Jane Kyle's murder. We want you to do an interview with the police about the shooting," Blake said to his son.

"I can't go there! They'll ask my name what do I say Mortimer's son or Blue Midnight's son! They will want to arrest me as a serial killer as Mortimer's son. Admitting I'm your son Midnight would make them suspect you are Mortimer and I am the Necromancer. They will arrest me?" said the Necromancer.

"Lie! give them a false name!" Max said, "It works me and Astra have done it before!" "Come off it Max nobody will believe the Necromancer saying-" the necromancer said.

"Hello, I am Merlin Starfire the reaper who took Jenny Kyle for processing!" said the Necromancer in a black-cowled monks robe as a skeleton."Hello Merlin!" said Simon, "come with me we need to do the interview in the-" "I know! Lead the way," said the Necromancer.

"This way," said Simon leading him to an interview room in it sat Blue Midnight and the masked Max."Max, I have brought you a relative!" said Simon. Max looked nervous, not sure if their trick backfired."It's fine Max!" the Necromancer said in Max's head, causing Max to calm down.

"Good morning, Mr grim reaper," said Max aloud.

"His name is Starfire too, Merlin Starfire," said the amused Simon.

"I told you we should have used another name!" said the Necromancer in Blake's mind."You needed to distract Uncle Sie he's clever," said Blake in his son's head."You should start the interview, Uncle Sie," said Blake aloud."Ok, let's go! sit down Merlin," said Simon. The reaper sat down.

Simon pressed the button of his recording device.

"Sergeant Simon Xander-Drax, Blue Midnight and The Sun King. Interviewing grim reaper Merlin Starfire. A witness in the murder of Jenifer Jane Kyle," Simon said, "Merlin Starfire is your name!" "So I am told," said the reaper offhandedly.

"You are told?" said Simon suspiciously;

"I am who I am called I have to go soon! Hurry up!" said the reaper.

"Do you have an appointment with a dying person," said Simon.

"No my daughter has a parent-teacher meeting! Of course, I have to take a soul for processing," the reaper said.

"You have no appointments with souls," Blake said in his son's mind.

"I have, I'm taking my soul for processing I can't be here long they know me!" the reaper said in Blake's mind.

"Calm down boy, he's just nervous," said Blake aloud.

"It's a boy! How do you know Its a skeleton," asked Simon.

"The bone structure is male about 25 years old, or he is one of us aliens who doesn't age beyond 25! For god's sake, his name is Merlin it is a male name!" Blake said aloud.

"Calm down everyone this is ridiculous! The way you're acting you'd think you were conspiring!" said Simon.

That woke up the necromancer's defiant side."What have I to hide I am completely transparent!" said the reaper. Simon laughed, he got the joke he was a skeleton you can see through bone holes.

"We can do our interview now!" said the reaper; "Ok your name is Merlin Starfire," said Simon."Yes," said the reaper."Did you see the victim die?" asked Simon."Yes!" the Reaper said."Can you say anything other than yes?" Blake asked.

"Yes," said the reaper chuckling.

"Why were you there?" asked Simon.

"To take the victim for processing in the afterlife, I am a grim reaper it is my purpose!" the reaper said.

"What did you see, for Argent sake!" Simon said.

"What has the fate Argent got to do with this!" asked the reaper laughing thinking of his boss trying to murder a man, he couldn't do it. The Necromancer was his assassin. Argent made the Necromancer kill people on a list of those who deserved to die because they were so evil. Blake saw his son as a serial killer as did the law. The Necromancer was his assassin.

"I didn't want to bring God into it!" said Simon."Who did I see killing the victim," asked Lance, the Necromancer."Exactly," said Simon."The killer, of course!" said Lance."Yes, who was it?" asked Simon frustrated."The Necromancer!" said Lance."What!" cried Blake.

"I wouldn't put it past him, but this isn't his modus operandi," Simon said frowning. Lance laughed. "Your him," said Simon angrily. "Yes I am but you can't do anything to me, I know your victim's true killer!" Lance said."You knew who he was Blake," Simon said biting his lip.

"Yes, I was told but I didn't see him as Captain Kamikaze!" Blake said disappointingly.

"Hey, what do you think I am The Masked Chicken! I couldn't take the tension!" said Lance defiantly. Lance's lawyer looked angry with his client. He was the Masked Chicken, otherwise known as Captain Kamikaze. He was an idiot who thought he was a superhero. He always got in trouble and had to be saved by the real heroes of the town including Max and Blake.

"It was not the Masked Chicken he was with me!" shouted the lawyer.

"Settle down Gabriel nobody is accusing you of anything!" Simon said.

The lawyer was blatantly the Chicken.

"I am not the Masked Chicken! He's a friend!" said Gabriel fixing his glasses which were the wrong prescription. They magnified his eyes greatly.

"I see how lame that sounds now!" Lance who'd once used the same excuse said.

"I knew we should have used my Mum as our lawyer and not do Gabriel a favor!" snapped Blake. "Can we please get back to the case!" screamed Simon.

Everyone else was startled.

"Who was the killer and don't say it was you!" Simon said.

"David Sebastian King," said Lance.

"How do you know his name," asked Simon.

"He was on fate's list of those to die he was to die for this crime!" said Lance.

"Oh! we'll arrest him," said Simon, "and you don't kill anyone!"

"Can't promise that, " said Lance.

"Go or I'll arrest you!" Simon shouted.

"Uncle-!" said Blake.

"All of you!" screamed Simon.

"But I am your Emperor!" Blake said.

"You are aiding and abetting a serial killer!" said Simon.

"Goodbye then!" said Blake, "If I am then I say come with me Necromancer and Sun King!" they dematerialized.

Elsewhere moments later! "Ok, who brought the Chicken!" Lance snapped seeing their lawyer was with them."Hey, I brought me!" said the offended Chicken, "let's go fight crime!" "Send me to hell please," begged Lance who hated the place. "We are now seen as criminal as he is! If we try to fight anything the police will arrest us!" Blake said, "Whatever and whoever we are!"

"They won't arrest us you are the emperor of the solar system," said the Chicken."I am nothing to do with the law's of man!" said Blake."How do we ditch the chicken, Dad," asked Lance."Dad? you are the son of Mortimer!" said the Chicken. Blake, Max, and Lance looked awkward."You have 2 dads?" asked the Chicken."Err! No, he's as old as my dad so I call him dad!" said Lance knowing it was a lame answer only an idiot would believe."I see!" said the Chicken believing him."All we can do is hide out until we can clear our names and I can't see that happening soon!" Blake said.

"Thanks to the zombie master we are now stuck in hiding we will need to somehow clear our names for knowing him!" Max said.

"You deserve it! You are a vampire!" said the Chicken.

"I'm a vampire! What does that matter?" Max said, "and you are an id-"

"Max no don't speak you'll only make matters worse!" Blake said putting his hand over Max's mouth stifling his words.

"Oh, how could you Max!" shouted the Chicken, "Stop looking surprised! I am a sorcerer too, I can read minds as well as you can!" "Forgot that!" Blake said."Are we going to continue to bicker or are we going to do something!" Lance said.

"Right boy we should get out of here we are too obvious shouting at each other someone must have heard us!" Blake said."We can hide out in Mort's office he is away on duty I believe!"

"Right Dad- err Midnight," said Lance awkwardly.

"You are the Limo driver Necromancer," Blake said."One, two, three!" said Lance on three the room disappeared and a Gothic office full of paperwork with a desk and a closet appeared around them. "Does Mortimer really write with a quill?" the Chicken asked, seeing a quill and ink on the desk.

"Yes," Blake said sadly.

"I was asking the Necromancer how would you know?" laughed the Chicken.

"He does!" Lance said.

"It looks a bore!" said Blake with the sound of one who knew only too well.

"No it looks fun!" said the Chicken, Blake moaned. A reaper walked in."Is that Mort?" the Chicken chirped seeing the reaper."No, he's Mort's assistant," Lance said.

"What is the mortal doing here?" asked Morton the reaper knowing full well who he was but he was out of place there. "What do you want Mort?" asked Lance. "A spirit needs judging they are waiting outside," said Morton.

"Max show the Masked Chicken the cupboard please," asked Blake."Let me show you this room!" Max said leading the Chicken to the cupboard."It looks very dingy!" said the Chicken entering it. Blake hid under the desk up stood Mortimer, "Show them in!" Mortimer croaked.

"Yes son," said Morton, the reaper soul of Blake's father as he left, taking in a soul Blake knew.

"He's been Judged already, why is he here?" croaked Mortimer.

"Hello cousin," the soul of Blake's arch enemy said.

"He's surely not here for good behavior!" hissed Mortimer.

"No, he killed two reapers and his cellmate! I didn't know it was even possible to do that, but he did!" said Morton."Merlin, the dark sorcerer can't help it, he is a bad seed," Mortimer said. "How is my daughter Astra?" Merlin asked Mortimer "Did you raise her Blake? She"was young when her mother and I were murdered," said Merlin,

"No, I did," Lance said.

"You! Why I thought you were a killer and you didn't have a paternal bone in your body!" said Merlin.

"Things change," said Lance.

"I take it you had children and you have not stopped killing," laughed Merlin.

"What do you take him for a saint?" said Mortimer.

"He could never be a saint his halo would fall off," said Merlin. walking around the table.

"True!" Mortimer said and laughed.

"It's dark in here I'm leaving," said The Chicken reacting quick Mortimer ran to the door holding it closed. The Chicken couldn't see him like that as Mortimer and his leader dead even he would guess the truth that Blake was Mortimer.

"Thank you for the body," Blake heard his voice say he looked to see his body dematerializing and

Merlin was gone.

"Damn!" said Mortimer. casting a locking spell on the door and moving back into the center of the room.

"What do we know?" Lance asked."Hope he's arrested as me! He's hidden his location," said Mortimer "I have to make some calls," said Mortimer pulling a black Mobile phone out of his desk, "Hello, this is a tip watch Astra Starfire to find Blue Midnight," said Mortimer on the phone then he hung up."Hello, Astra, the police are watching you! Your dad stole my body! Let the police arrest him," Mortimer said in his second call.

"All we have to do now is wait!" Mortimer told Lance and Morton.

"Blake I caught you at last!" Simon said in the police station to the captured body of Blake with Merlin inside him. "How dare you arrest me, I am the emperor of-" boasted Merlin." Maybe, but that has no legal merit I can arrest any criminal!" said Simon."Blake is a criminal?" asked Merlin. and paused and said, "Look, I'm not Blake I just stole his body!" "Yeah right who are you the dark sorcerer Merlin?" asked Simon laughing."Yes!" said Merlin, who was having a fit."Pull the other rabbit!" said Simon.

"Mortimer is Blake's soul," said Merlin.

"Very unlikely you are here so is he," said Simon.

"I came to take friend Blake to an appointment he is late!" said Mortimer.

"He's Blake!" said Merlin pointing at Mortimer excitedly.

"Oh yes of course I am and you are a body snatcher then," Mortimer laughed.

"I am! I am Merlin!" said Merlin.

"You can't be he's dead!" said Simon, "If you need him you take him, I can't stop a reaper!" Simon said and that was how Blake got his body back. The mad sorcerer Merlin was furious in his cell in solitary confinement forever more. Blake and Max enchanted the recording so it only said what they wanted. Lance, otherwise known as the Enchanter whipped and rearranged the mind of Simon. So they were seen as innocent as the Masked Chicken who was so innocent, he got in tons of trouble but enough of him.

"Blake it's dark in here and I'm scared of the dark! Let us out of here! Max, stop looking at me like that! You'd think I was food!" the trapped Chicken cried.

"I like Chicken!" said Max.

The Chicken screamed and fainted.

"Finally some peace! What does he take me for!" Max said laughing.

The Magicians: The Spirits of the Land

The Magicians: The Spirits of the Land
The Zigzag man

"Ew! that is disturbing," said the wife of the magician Blake Alexander. Blake was performing the zigzag man for real on stage in a small theatre in Princetown near Dartmoor in England. He was a noted Australian stage magician on a tour of England.

"It's only a trick Mrs. Alexander," said the owner of the theatre who sat next to her. Mrs. Alexander knew it was real not a stage trick.

"Max hurry up I'm bleeding to death. Put me back together. I smell a reaper in the audience," Blake Alexander said. He was literally beside himself. Because he was a real magician, not just a stage one.

"That's is your son! He's the reaper in the audience" said Max Starfire said in Blake's head laughing.

" Hi Lance," said Max out loud waving to Lance who was enjoying seeing his dad in that awkward position. Obviously, they didn't like each other.

Lance waved back smiling.

"Max is enjoying this," Lance laughed.

"He's not the only one," said Mrs. Alexander glaring at her stepson.

"Do you want me to put him together again?" Max shouted aloud.

"No don't he'll have more of him to do his paperwork!" cried the amused Lance.

"Max!" Screamed Blake who was dying.

"Ok! Ok! You win Blake," Max conceding said as he put Blake back together and removing the blades. Then opened the door out stepped Blake in one piece.

"You nearly had a special guest the grand reaper Mortimer you creep! Trust a vampire to do a dangerous trick what should I expect!" Blake hissed in Max's head.

"Blake is a good sport!" said Max to the audience.

"with a baseball bat!" Lance said.

"This brings us to the end of the show!" said Blake glaring at his son.

The magicians took their bows

Tea and other conspiracies

"Max tried to kill me that is the last time we do that trick!" Blake said in a small cafe in Princetown.

"No I didn't I was playing to the crowd!" said Max Starfire.

"Right playing to the crowd my son wants my job
so you left me to die!" said Blake shortly.

"I didn't kill you Blake stop acting like a drama queen," Max snapped.

"Waiter where are our teas?" Lance called out.

"Your Devonshire teas are on the way," a nearby waiter said.

"Thanks," Lance chirped back.

Moments later another waiter came back with a tray with the meals.

"What is that?" asked Lance furiously.

"Your meals!: said the waiter;

"Calm down boy," Blake said.

"But it's wrong!" Lance said.

"How?" asked the waiter who was scared Lance had the look of a killer.

"the cream is on the scone and the jam is on the cream!" said Lance.

"Yes!" said the waiter nervously.

" the cream goes on the jam!" Lance snapped.

"That is not right here!" said the waiter.

"Down Necromancer he's not one of your victims!" Blake snapped.

"But-" Lance said..

"No buts stop playing with your food!" Blake said.

Lance looked sheepish he knew who was boss.

"Sorry we are foreigners we don't understand your ways," said Blake.

The waiter served them and ran off.

"Angela and Astra.are going to be shopping today what should we do?" asked Max.

"I want to investigate the mysteries of Dartmoor," said Lance.

"Me too!" Blake said.

"You just want to read your book you're reading the Hound of the Baskervilles," Lance said.

"It's a good book," said Blake.

"I want to find out if there are aliens and ghosts on the moors," said Lance.

"If we go there we'll find them us! We're aliens! As for ghosts they are not there! They are on the

other side," said Blake, "you know that Lance we're grim reapers Lance we take them there."
"There are witnesses lets investigate them," said Lance.
All but Blake were convinced there were aliens out there on the moor.

Saints and mortals
"I can't believe you talked me into going here!" Blake moaned, as he wandered the moors of Dartmoor with a stick to test the ground for mires. He was looking for moss and solid ground.
"Put a rabbit in it, Blake," snapped Max.
"Why are you flying It's only a moor, not a comic book!" Blake snapped back at Max who was floating a meter over the ground.
"I'm not flying," said Lance offended.
"You! Your walking on water!" Blake said exasperatedly.
Lance was the standing on the moor on a deep dangerous part as if it was as stable as solid ground. There was noise nearby.
Multiple clicks.
"What's that noise?" asked Lance looking for the source of it.
They saw a man taking photos of them with a phone.
To the horror of the Photographer, something impossible happened
Max, Blake, and Lance disappeared into thin air.

Blake, Lance, and Max materialized in in the center of a circle of rocks a Tor.
"You hear that aliens have been sight here," Lance said.
"Yes, they have I know!" Blake said.
"Nice to see you not being negative," Lance said, "What do suppose they were X-zercien?"
"Us! common or garden Zodiacs!" Blake said, "we were photoed!"
"Don't say we! I can't be photoed I am a vampire!" Max said.
"Ok so they got a picture of me and the second coming!" said Blake "I don't need Angela seeing it she banish me to hell again." Blake moaned.
"Lucky for me no one knows me here," Lance said.
"Your step mum will ground you too!" Max laughed.
"mum can't do that I am an adult," Lance said.
"She is the wife of the emperor of the solar system and the king of the grim reapers she can do anything," Max said.
"What about you not showing up in the picture!" Lance said.
"What of that?" said Max offhandedly.
"I raised your wife, my niece! She says vampires shouldn't draw attention to the fact they're vampires!" Lance said, "She won't find it funny either!"
They walked the moors awhile longer. that was until Blake started seeing a giant black hell hound. Which he decided to hunt. None of the others saw it and Max pointed out it was not real and Blake had been sniffing to much swamp gas.

Later back in Princetown in their hotel, they were staying in the Harrabeer Country House. The men caught up with Angela and Astra who'd been shopping while the men were on the moor.
"Have you seen this," asked Angela pushing paper in front of them. "In the paper, there are tales of flying men on the moor! They even a photo. Speculations were that they were ghost or aliens," Angela snapped.
"I wasn't doing anything unusual," Blake snapped back.
"Max how could you betray our people the vampires so blatantly," Astra scolded.
"Me I'm not in the picture!" Max retorted self-righteously.
"They saw you and saw you not in the picture you proved our existence!" Astra said.

"They think I'm a ghost of swamp gas," Max said, " no harm in that,"
"I suppose not," said Astra.
"Blake can testify to swamp gas making you see things he tried to hunt a dog who wasn't there!" Max laughed.
"Blake!" Angela said turning to him.
"It was real! I saw it!" Blake protested.
"why did he see a dog?" Astra asked.
"He's reading the hound of the Baskervilles," Lance said.
Blake could see why it was relevant the others laughed.

Scion of Death

"Nocturne or the music of the night The night is like music it is cool and crisp, smooth and elegant, the stars twinkle like music, the moon sails across the sky like a music score, the darkness is the like beat of the heart listening to music or looking in the mystery which is the night, the night enthrals like a sweet riff of music, the beauty of the night is the music of the stars, the ghostly light of night is like an aria soft, a song of the night is the unearthly glow, the ethereal atmosphere of night is like a favorite song, night tugs on the heart string like a beautiful voice in song, it is the music of the night." recited a nervous student, Kristine Alexander to her class. some were impressed some were just bored as they were in a literature class at school. Some others hated poetry as much as school. "Nice reading Kris you did a good job," her teacher said. "That was amazing Kris," her best friend Mika said when she got back to her seat.

Elsewhere at the school, the principal looked green. "More paperwork!" grumbled a man in a lab coat and suit in glasses. "A student dies at my kids' school and you moan about paperwork," a man in a blue tux and mask in a top hat snapped. "Sorry boy but this is the tenth murder and the paperwork is piling up. "The Enchanter has children here?" the principal asked. "Yes Kristine and Lance Alexander Jnr," said the man in the lab coat as he sniffed the air. "Do you have a cold?" the principal asked. "No, I smell-! no matter" the man in the lab coat said. "Dr. Alexander the school isn't safe. We can't hide it anymore the people here and their families need to know," said the principal. "Yes," replied Dr. Blake Alexander straightening his glasses. The principal left to organize an assembly. "What did you smell, dad?" the Enchanter asked. "A black wraith!" said Blake looking seriously put out because they were more paperwork for him. "I smelt something dead and evil something dangerous the killer no doubt! I have never come across a wraith before what are they like?" "You!" snapped Blake, "They are like you!" The Enchanter rolled his eyes he was used to being called a monster by his dad. "No what are they really like," the Enchanter said. "Evil! dark creatures monsters!" said Blake. "Ok they're like me but why is it killing at random?" said the Enchanter. "It has no self-control!" said Blake, "And it is angry!" "why?" said the Enchanter. "How should I know ask your brother! He sees all!" snapped Blake. "I am going to get my children!" said the Enchanter. A few minutes later a man stood at the door of Kristine's class. He heard someone reading he listened and smiled proudly.

"The Shadow of the Wind under the moon's silver glow I heard the wind blow the autumn leaves flew past me, like silver charms in night's debris,

the wind it cools, the night was full of the airs of scented jewels, the breeze blew on the lake causing ripples of silver and shadow, I hear the wind's cries and see its tears which fly and show, as silver glowing rain, it is the coming of a storm, the shadows of the wind do form, where the shadow of the wind does go the silver aura of night shows in its glow," Kristine read.

"That was good Kris," said the teacher. The man knocked on the door. The teacher walked to it and opened it she saw a tall handsome young man in a black business suit. "Hello, what do you want?" the teacher asked. "Hello, I am Lance Alexander I came for my daughter," said the man. "Why has she an appointment? why didn't she tell me before?" said the teacher hardly believing he was old enough to be her father he looked 25 she was 18. "what proof do you have that you are her father?" the teacher said not convinced. "I am older than I look!" said Lance, "Hi Kristine how are you going in there?" "Great dad why are you here now?" asked Kristine. "On business, granddad is here too!" said Lance. from behind Lance stepped Blake still in his lab outfit. "Whose he meant to be your brother?" asked the teacher. "Hey Granddad," said Kristine seeing him. "Hello Kristine," said Blake. "You've got to be kidding me he's as old as you are?" the teacher snapped, "Kris is not going anywhere with you jokers." "There is going to be an announcement over the loudspeakers, Mrs. Croft!" said Blake. Then over the loudspeakers came the voice of the principal he was calling for the school to assemble. "How did you know that and who I was?" the teacher asked. "while we were at the office to find out where Kristine was they told us about the assembly," Blake said. "How can I prove I am her father you think we're a joke!" Lance said. "Come boy let 's go to the assembly," said Blake. "Class we're going to the assembly," the teacher said. All went there. "Kris who were those strange men?" asked Mika suspicious. "My dad and granddad!" said Kristine in reply. "We have to sadly inform you that we have a killer in the school!" the Principal said. "I know who it is," shouted Mrs. Croft, "Who?" cried Mika, "Who is it Mrs. Croft?" voices asked she turn to Lance and Blake and pointed at Lance. "Just what I need!" snapped Lance rolling his eyes. "No!" said the principal into the mic, "That is Kristine and Lance Alexander Jnr's father. If I'm not mistaken and the coroner," "told you," said Lance. Mrs. Croft looked confused. "Dad granddad hi," shouted Jnr seeing them. Blake waved, Lance smiled. There were lots of confused people the looked too young to be their grandfather and father. "Look it is Blake Fire the magician," a voice shouted everyone looked for the famous stage magician. Blake Laughed. "Max! very funny!" Blake said he was him. Max was his partner in the stage act. "You two fighting yet?" asked Max walking to them. "What brings you here?" asked Blake. "I'm the cleaner, community service," said Max. "Oh," said Blake.

"I've seen some of the crime scene as such," Max said. "You cleaning the scenes?" asked Lance. "Yes," Max said looking grim. "Max is my assistant!" Blake said, "In all things he is my assistant on the case. So anyone who has information of needs help tell him and I'll find out and or come to help you." "I'm not your assistant I'm your partner, Dead Head!" Max hissed. "Whatever you say, Max!" Blake retorted. "Please not now you two this is a school. We don't need you fighting like school boys," Lance snapped seeing a big argument about to start. Max rolled his eyes. "School boys! I am -" Blake snapped interrupted by Lance. "An arrogant over puffed police man!" Lance snapped. Blake realised he was being a bit over bearing for a coroner. "Sorry Max, Lance come with me," Blake said looking serious. Lance and Max followed him out of the room. "I still can't believe that man is not a killer," the teacher said "he looks like a killer." Kristine laughed who knew he was secretly a killer The feared Necromancer. "What are you laughing at Kristine?" said the teacher suspiciously. Later elsewhere in the school. "Could the wraith be the Necromantix? She is new to the school, she appeared at the same time as the wraith did," Lance said. "Maybe or she is a fan of you," Blake said like a barb. "She may be a copycat," Max said. "I smelt women's perfume as well as a wraith at the murder scene," Blake said, "It is very likely female." A teen aged girl in black was walking in the cloak of darkness with a slightly younger teen age girl also in black. "Kris Is this the Crime scene?" the younger girl asked. "Yes Mika my Father keeps good paper work. I stole some of it without his knowing," Kristine said a folder materialised in her left hand. "What does it say?" asked Mika Davenport. "The suspect is the a dark wraith to be the killer," said Kristine skimming through the report. "A what? You have got to be kidding they don't exist!" said Mika in disbelief. "They are real I met one once wasn't very nice," said Kristine. "what are they like?" asked Mika curiously. "Dark shadowy creatures with a liking to do harm to people," said Kristine flicking to the next page. "We shouldn't be here! they suspect me of being the wraith!" Kristine said abruptly. "Oh no!" Mika said panicking. Suddenly Kristine and Mika's clothes changed to school Uniforms. "How?" asked Mika taken aback. "They are coming!" said Kristine making the file disappear. "Kristine what are you doing here?" said Blake entering the room seeing her wear she should not be. "What are you doing here?" Lance said with the air of a father. "I was investigating the scene of the last death," Kristine said. "What?" said Lance. "How did you know where it was we haven't told anyone," said Blake. "I stole a police file!" Kristine said. "Why?" Lance asked. "You guys need help from an insider," said Kristine. "What use is a young enchantress this is adult work!" Lance said offhandedly then asked "why did you bring your friend Mika with you?" "How dare you endanger a human!" Max said. "She is helping me," said Kristine. Mika looked nervously at Blake. "Are you alright?" Blake asked her. "I am alright," said Mika nervously. "What a strange girl," Blake thought. "She's not strange granddad she's my friend," Kristine said reading his mind. Blake smiled. "Sorry," Blake said. "Send her home," Lance said, "This killer will go after her if she's mixed up in this, she has no powers to defend herself." "Dad's right, Mika you are endangering your self mixing with us," Kristine said. "Ok I'll go," Mika said too eagerly still looking through Blake she left. "Why is she scared of Blake?" Max said. "I couldn't read her," Lance said. "She's not scared of anyone," Kristine protested. "It was as if she knew who I am!" Blake said. "She doesn't know you are the king of the Grim reapers. She also doesn't even know that you are the Necromancer, Dad," Kristine said shortly. There was a blood curdling scream nearby. "It's struck again," Blake said they all disappeared into thin air like ghosts. They reappeared in front of the victim and the wraith. "What are yoU?" asked the wraith spooked. "Blue Midnight, The Enchanter. The King of the Sun, and The Enchantress!" Blake said. "We came to avenge your victims," said Lance a sword materialised in his hand. "I am a ghost swords don't hurt me!" said the Wraith laughing. "I feel naked without my sword," said Lance. "Anything to keep you clothed," the Wraith laughed. Lance flashed it a look that spoke daggers. Blake was frustrated he came as Blake and not a reaper. He would endanger his body if he became a reaper. He felt stifled and in control as crab being cooked alive in a pot. "Be gone!" said Kristine said in a voice no dead thing could resist. The Wraith disappeared. So did Max. "Vampires!" Blake hissed rolling his eyes. "I forgot Max was a vampire," laughed Kristine. "The King of Vampires is dead so he had to do what you said," Blake said. "Wonder where they when?" said Lance. "Honey are you alright?" Max's wife Astra seeing him appear in their home in a trance. He didn't reply. "Max!" she said. "You have no power over me Life is mine, yours is death, I am life, you are death, death has no power over life I thus am as strong as you." read Kristine in literature class the next day. "nicely read Kristine," her teacher said. "Kristine, where is Mika she is not a school today," her teacher asked her later. "I don't know!" Kristine said, "I think she is trying to keep out of the way of the killer." "She should be at school even if there is killer the police are at school," said the teacher frowned, "can't blame her." Later that day she found out why her friend was not at school she was dead murdered by the Wraith. "Well hello, Nectomantrix," said a voice behind Kristine. "what?" Kristine cried spining round to see the speaker. It was Mika! Or was it? "How?" Kristine said looking at the body and the speaker. "I'm caught and you are dead!" said the ghost. Kristine screamed. Max materialised. "I can't fight a ghost!" Max said, "I'll get help! Necromancer, Mortimer come here The Wraith has me and Kristine!" Moments later. A grim reaper materialised with a man in black with sword and a mask appeared. "You!" said the Wraith glaring at the reaper. "Me?" the reaper hissed. "I saw through your disguise!" said the wraith. "I see." Mortimer said. "Max ignore me." Mortimer said to the vampire. "Happily," Max said. "You wraith come with Me you are late with your appointment with the afterlife!" Mortimer said. Leading the Wraith away for processing in the other world. "Hello Dad thanks for coming," said Kristine. "Hello Kris you did a good job finding the Wraith. Sorry about your friend," The Necromancer said hugging his daughter, "You are a very girl. The Necromantrix was posing as your friend for a week it seems Mika was dead for a week by the smell of her!"

"No It was not the Necromantrix I am the Necromantrix," said Kristine pulling away. "Oh Then you-" said The Necromancer. "Borrowed my father's name," said Kristine interrupting, "I wanted to help you solve the case."

"We couldn't have solved it without you." said the Necromancer.

Time out of time

People are always talking time with me. I am a lord of time, not a Dr Who Time Lord. I don't travel in time policing the time locked people. I am more time locked that they are, I am stuck in a dimension out of time's influence. I watch time go by in my pool of time a scrying pond of pure liquid time.

I seldom actually meet anyone but I know what is happening in time like a man watching the news on television.

The events of time are my only channel in my pond.

Shame would like to check out Dr Who! But I'm an enchanter, not a temporal physicist and electrician. so I don't get television channels.

On time travel I am an expert. I know every portal to every moment in time and on occasion send people on errands in the past of future to them. One such one occurred last week to me but 5 months ago to all other concerned you may not remember but the moon hatched. I sent my father and brother to fix it in the distant past. I should explain the Moon only hatched because a giant space locust laid an egg in it. It hatched breaking the moon to pieces in its birth.

The species are known planet killers. So I had to send them back to the time of the laying of the seed of destruction for the moon. Because without the moon the earth dies. I could do nothing. Well anyway, they as the descendants of the kings of the Sun had the power of the Sun in them.

Even though they fight like cats and dogs. They were the only ones who could incinerate the mother and destroy the egg which would hatch millennia later. The locust race has an allergy to starfire which makes them explode. I was asked by my brother why can we change the past in that time and not in the instance of saving our murdered mother from being murdered in the past. I said it was a fixed point in time which it was she was meant to die and be reincarnated. Time is complected of chance and happenstance. Very rarely seeing what is to come can prove there are some things that are just meant to be.

Elysium Fields

I wander alone for a while in paradise,
the sun beats warmly on my back,
I smell the ripening hay,
I feel the grasses on my hand forget life the world and all,
the hay brushes softly against my clothes,
causing a sweet shushing sound,
I open my eyes and see my bony hand and black robes,
another reaper walks up to me,
I lose my dream of Elysium I realize I'm late for work and I must return
to my office to judge the dead as is my job.

The Necromantix and the Necromancer

"You aren't my boss you are my daughter," the Necromancer said to the one who gave Fate his hit list to give to him.
"What is it you can't take that I'm a teenager or your daughter?" snapped back the Necromantric as sharp as her father's sword he killed with.
"You are you! You shouldn't be caught up in murder," the Necromancer said, " I know if I am caught I will have hell to pay I don't want it for you."
"no more than you are," the Necromantric said.
"This is serious It is no child's game people die. What do you think this is Death Note?" said the Necromancer.
"I know now of us can speak Japanese!" the Necromantrix retorted.
"This no joke!" the Necromancer said shortly.
"I never thought it was," the Necromanctrix said.
"I was hoping it was!" said a man tied up in a chair.
"You! I'll deal with you later!" said The Necromancer turning to his latest victim. who would be dead as all the Necromancer's victims.
Causing him to be a serial killer. He had found out his daughter wrote fate's list of people to die his kill list. to say he wasn't happy would be an underestimation of the case. He didn't know what to do or say to stop her endangering herself, fate and himself of being in trouble with the police

The Masked Chicken Vs. The Vampires

The Masked Chicken once hunted vampires,
scary thoughts it inspires,
it was a travesty,
no great mystery,
he was an idiot who thought he was a hero,
his saves total to zero,
he hunted the vampires' king and queen,

it was easier than it did seem.
they hid never,
he had no chance whatsoever,
he ran up to them with a stake,
his idea was one that he did only half bake,
the queen grabbed the stake and knocked him out,
when he awoke and could not find them about.

And Then Darkness Fell

The fading ghost of daylight,
Dissolves into the night,
The ghostly light of the night starts it's haunting,
The eye it's taunting,
To look and see,
What in it be." recited the Necromantrix as she played with her victim.
"Why are you reciting Poetry," her father the Necromancer asked.
"Why not?" said the Necromantix,
"You are trying to murder him not seduce him," said the necromancer.
"I may be a teenager but I know the difference," the Necromantrix said.
She pulled her knife away from victims neck, She had been tracing it across their body flirtatiously.
"Stop playing with your food," said the Necromancer shortly.
"Food! Are you a vampire?" the victim said.
"No," the Necromantrix retorted.
"She's my apprentice," the Necromancer said,
"The Necromancer has an apprentice serial killer?" said the confused the victim who was in love
with his torturer and scared of her.
"I am not a serial killer I am the right hand of Fate!" the Necromancer said frustratedly he read
minds he knew the teenaged boy who was his daughter's age, the boy liked her and was sickened.
"Kill him or I will," snapped the father.
"I will in my way," said the daughter.
"You have no way!" said the Necromancer.
She kissed the boy he fell down dead,
The Necromantrix lower her arm holding her now bloody knife.
"That was disgusting!" said her father,
"Not as messy as you!" said a grim reaper walking in the room,
:"Dad, hi!" said the Necromancer. to the reaper.
"I distracted him while I cut his throat," said the Necromantrix.
"I appreciate that I won't have to do DNA and tooth tests to identify them as coroner you aren't
going to mince him are you Necromancer?" asked the reaper who was the local coroner.
"No!" said the Necromancer shortly..
"It was my kill," said the Necromantrix.
"You 2 are sick," said the reaper hitting his head.
"Maybe but you look a horror!" said the Necromancer, "why are you here to Insult us?"
"No I am here to take you victim to the other side!" said the reaper.
"Do your job and stop bothering me I'm feeling sick," said the Necromancer.
"You work makes me sick!" said the reaper,
"Go you have paperwork to do," said the Necromancer.
"Oh yeah I forgot the ghost, Got to dash hell won't wait!" said the reaper taking the ghost of the

victim and left the Necromancer throwing up in a bucket which materialized in his hands. While his
daughter looked sorry for him.

Masquerade of the Vampires

Astra queen of vampires went to a masquerade,
opportunist, she was with her husband Max, the king,
they danced all night, then they got people alone and they
took a little drink
She savored the taste of the blood she drank,
she drank it in a wine glass in her black-gloved hand. Her gloves were of fishnet lace her hands
bejeweled.
her husband stood admiring her long black tresses, her dress, and
her gothic beauty,
Her mask a black lace mask fit tight on her finely chiseled face. Max told a joke. She laughed and
cried she laughed too much. She flirting with silence bit her fingertips. They danced like newlyweds
enjoying the dance and each other's company. Their eyes never left each other It was as if nothing
else mattered, their hearts in their mouths, the world felt like as if it was theirs alone. They took joy
in each other's touch and movements and the other's loving glance. The world was lost all that
existed was the music and the magical moment which lasted till the dawn's light peaked in and the
moment was gone.

Ghost in the school

There was a wraith in the the school of the scion of death,
It was feared by all with every breath,
Death and his son were on the case,
They were suspected all over the place,
Death's granddaughter came into her own,
Her powers of magic had grown,
She found the wraith who killed,
In the place of dead friend it filled,
It caught her she was lost,
The janitor found her, he was her father's friend the king of fire and frost,
He could not assist so he went for help,
Death and son returned as reaper king and the Necromancer the ghost was beaten he did yelp,
The reaper king took the ghost for processing,
While son hugged his daughter calling her brave reflecting.

The Ice Queen of Pluto extended

Astra the queen of Pluto,
she was the daughter of the dark king of Pluto she lost her parents young she cannot let go,
she is the queen of ice wife of the sun king,
she only sorrow does bring,
she is the queen of vampires too,
she lives in the daylight with little ado,
she is of the grand reaper's decent.
so she's a necromancer that's what I meant.
she wears sometimes a lacy gown of white,
and a white wig long blue makeup on her pale skin with a crown of ice when she goes out at night.

Ballad of the Necromancer

I am of an alien sorcerer race,
we all look like young adults even the old ones of our race,
we live forever but for accidents, we die,
I am the Necromancer,
a killer of man,
I hate to kill but it is my lot in life,
I am the assassin of fate,
I kill those on his list of people to die,
I am an enchanter too,
as one I am seen in a better light,
they see me as a hero and a villain,
I see me in a complicated light,
I am what I am,
I do what I do,
for the good of my family and the empires of life and death.

The Dark Realm

Elysian is the realm of the dead,
I am it's king it is a very dark place
and it smells to high heavens!
it reeks of death and hopelessness,
the office area is large and Gothic,

made of wood and stone,
I am the king of the grim reapers,
they call me the grand reaper,
the outer parts are dark and dismal tunnel-like corridors to the smaller rooms and cells.
the reapers are its guards and bureaucrats who run it.
no one ever escapes from the other side to return to the land of life,
except for my wife who was reincarnated illegally.
she came back to the land of life.

The Necromantrix

The Power of life,
the power of death,
the power of love,
the power of hate
enchanting the eye,
enchanting the mind,
the dark soul of ages,
the light heart of time,
lady of destiny,
lady of the past,
the spirit of destruction,
the spirit of creation,
the child of death,
the child of life,
bringer of life,
bringer of death,
control of the living,
control of the dead.
an enchantress, a lady of life,
a necromantrix, a lady of death.

The Scent of Death

Ironically one may say I dislike my work as coroner and the grand reaper partly because the smell
of death lingers in both of my offices, it is a foul ripe smell of blood and rotting of corpses, the
coroner's office is slightly masked by chemicals and is slightly ventilated so the scent of death is
less extreme. In the land of the dead Elysian, It is like Death on steroids,
concentrated by the fact it is populated by the dead, making it even worse to bear.

Tempus, lord of time

Time is long,
time is lonely,
I watch time go by in my only companion the glowing pool of time
in it I see and hear lives and times in the empty tunnels of time my home in exile,
I am the loneliest of my race they call me Tempus, the Timekeeper, lord of time.

The Mysterious Dr. Death

"This is thankless job mine," moaned the local Coroner called Dr. Death by the people of the
hospital he worked.
"Yeah no one likes the messenger of bad tidings," said his assistant the only one there who liked
him luckily she was his wife or he would have no one there who understood him.
"Dr. Death we have another freshy for you," an orderly said walking in the morgue.
"How many time must I tell you not to refer to them as freshies!:" scalded Dr. Death.
The orderly handed him a folder and left.
"I hate that guy he has no respect for the dead," said Dr. Death.
"Some people don't," said his wife.
Blake read the folder and wandered off.

"Are you here for Kyle Charmers?" Dr. Death asked a group of people who were thinking about a
man called Kyle. Dr. Death read minds so knew they were the group he wanted.
"Yes, is he alright," asked the wife of Kyle.
"No I am afraid He died of complications in the operation," Dr. Death said as was his job there he
was the banshee of the hospital the one who reported to families when someone died.
Little did the people who called him Dr. Death know how right that name was.
"Morton what did you do with Kyle Chamers?" said Dr. Death seeing a grim reaper wandering
around the hospital.
"Oh him he refused to go so I used the voice on him," said the reaper.
"So that's why he was late for processing," muttered the doctor.
"Val is acting up again If only we could tell him the truth," said Morton.
"He always had a chip on his shoulder," said Dr. Death," Dad won't take being a puppet of a
necromancer well. He barely take being a zombie well."
"True," said Morton the reaper hugged Dr. Death.
"Bye, dad," said Dr. Death as the reaper soul of his father wandered off.
"What was that?" asked the orderly who saw the doctor hugging a grim reaper.
"None of your business," snapped Dr. Death, who wandered off leaving the orderly in shock.

The Blood Bank

"How is the blood drive going?" asked a doctor called Dr. Death at the local hosipital where he worked.

"Good," said Astra who ran it with her husband Max.

"It is bit odd?" said Dr. Death.

"What?" asked Astra.

"Vampires running a blood drive," said Dr. Death.

"We are doing this for a good cause," said Astra Queen of vampires.

"What you and Max get free feed on tap?" asked Dr. Death.

"No food for the poor vampires of Queenscross," said Astra.

"Blake how it going," asked her husband Max.

"Good," said Dr. Death, "you know the Red Fox will be up in arms If he realized this is for vampires."

"He's police to the bone," said Max, "Yeah but we aren't using our own names."

"The owner's of this Blood bank are dead," said Astra.

"Vampire victims?" Dr. Death asked.

"No a car crash," said Astra.

"Oh," said Dr. Death.

Later.

"Astra, I have had reports there is a blood bank ran by vampires for vampire running have you heard of it?" quizzed the Red Fox a sorcerer like herself he was her a few times great Uncle.

"No it is news to me," said Astra, "why don't I ever find these things! it sounds like someone's getting a free feed."

"It is sick!" said the Fox," and wrong on so many levels we must catch the instigators."

"If you say so," said Astra.

"Yes, this cannot be taken lightly or they'll think it's the norm," said the Fox.

Elsewhere a vampire raid on the blood bank was happening.

"This is enough nosh for a year," a vampire said to his vampire friend.

"I can't believe they left it unguarded," said the other.

They filled a truck with all the blood they stole and left wondering why they left the place unguarded to be robbed.

At the same time, Max was pulling a rabbit out of a hat on stage at a large theatre.

"Blake will now make me disappear," said Max walking into a box.

"If only," said Blake fed up of hearing the good the blood bank will do for the poor local vampires.

"Abracadabra!" Blake said posturing.

Then Blake opened the box and Max was gone.

He didn't come back to Blake's great frustration.

"Eh Max come on jokes over!" shouted Blake looking embarrassed and angry deserted in the middle of their magic act.

Max was at the empty blood bank looking angry enough to kill! The alarm going.

Later.

"We got the blood bank Vampires," said the Fox to Astra and Max went to pick her up from the police station.

"You have how who were there?" asked Max.

"Two scavengers," said the Fox, "they had the blood with them in the back of their truck."

"Truck?" said Astra confused.

"They robbed us dry must be the robbers," thought Max.

"They claimed they robbed the blood bank but that is doubtful. We won't investigate their claims!" said the Fox.

Astra understood now they had been robbed and the thieves would pay for their crimes in their place.

The Children of the Necromancer

"What is Super Dork doing here Mega Dork!" asked Kristine the daughter of the Necromancer.

"Hey quit with the super dork I'm your granddad," said Blake Alexander their father's Dad.

"He came for tea," said the Necromancer who was used to being called dork not Dad.

"Why you two hate each other," said Junior the son of the Necromancer.

"We share differing opinions but we're still family," said Blake.

"Yes," said his son.

"Hmm!" huffed Kristine.

"Lance I have a book I need you to destroy," said Blake.

"Now I'm in the business of burning books am I?"

asked the Necromancer laughing.

"I'd do it myself if it was that simple," said Blake offhandedly, "It is cursed,"

"Cursed really," said the Necromancer his face lightening up, "By who?"

"The dark king of Pluto," said Blake.

"Astra's father," said the Necromancer.

"No his father- of course, Astra's Dad your sister Valkira's husband. He cursed it before he died," hissed Blake.

"Ok, ok, don't bite my head off!" said the Necromancer.

"Will you destroy it or not?" Blake snapped.

"I will tonight," said the Necromancer.

Later while their father was arguing with his father his teenage children who thought they were mad as there was no such thing as magic let alone curses wanted to see the book which caused their elders to argue.

"This is the cursed book!" laughed Kristine looking at it.

"Bible of Necromancy," said Junior reading the title, and said nervously, "Maybe we should leave this alone."

"Wimp!" said Kristine picking up the book opening it.

She read a line from the book and the children were encompassed in darkness. Blinded they felt like they were falling forever til suddenly they were standing in a dark place.

"Where are we," asked Junior nervously.

"How should I know dork!" said Kristine.

A ghost walked up to them.

"You are not dead why are you here?" asked the ghost.

"Where are we?" asked Junior.

"the other side Elysian," said the ghost, "Are one you of them?"

"One of them? one of what?" asked Kristine.

"A Necromancer?" asked the ghost.

"Mega dork?" asked Kristine.

"Who me?" asked the ghost offended.

"No that's what we call our father he's a psycho killer called the Necromancer," said Junior, "he thinks he thinks he's a sorcerer!"

"You are the Necromancer's children!" said the ghost growing angry.

He tried to kill Kristine by throttling her.

"He killed me," said the ghost.

"Leave her alone and go away," said Junior in a voice which compelled the ghost to listen and do as he said.

"The Necromancer's brat is a necromancer!" cried the ghost fading into the darkness.

"Necromancer me? No!" said, Junior.

"You dork!" said Kristine hitting her brother.

After wandering aimlessly for a while they found and a door

"What is a door doing in the other world?" said Kristine.

"Let's open it we have nothing to lose," said Junior.

"We could find someone who hates Dad behind the door," said Kristine.

"I'll protect you!" said Junior.

He opened the door and found a Gothic old fashion stone and wood office full of paperwork.

"What are you doing in my office," demanded a skeleton in a black monks outfit behind them.

"Leave us you monster!" cried Kristine.

"You!" cried the grim reaper.

"Do you know us?" asked Kristine.

"Of course what I don't know is how you are here?" said the reaper.

"we read from a cursed book!" said Kristine.

"That lousy good for nothing!" the grim reaper moaned.

"Necromancer get your good for nothing lazy self here now!" screamed the reaper. Moments later he appeared a masked man in black wearing sword called doom.

"Look what I found roaming around down here!" shouted the reaper dressing down the masked man.

"Kristine and Junior oh my god!" cried the masked man hugging them he was in tears since seeing them,

"Mega Dork?" said Kristine not sure it was her father.

"Yes," said the Necromancer.

"Why are you here?" asked Junior.

"I was called here!" said the Necromancer.

"Who is he?" asked Kristine of the reaper.

The reaper walked into a cupboard out walked their grandfather, Blake.

"Super Dork?" asked Junior not believing his eyes.

"Yes it's me Grandad! Lance that girl of yours is a necromancer she used the voice on me Lance!" said Blake.

"A ghost called Junior a necromancer too!" said Kristine,"The ghost tried to kill me he told it to let me go and leave and it did!"

"Oh my god I'm so proud of you both," said the Necromancer.

"So your two powerless children took after you!" said Blake smiling hugging his grandchildren proudly.

Catch me if you can

"I'm worried the world has gone mad! Death has been corrupted by fate to protect his son from fate and the fate has started to kill it is not good for either of them, neither is this corruption," said

Tempus

the Timekeeper to a sorcerer he knew.

"What can I do?" asked the sorcerer, "I'm worried too."

"Take this list and do fate's will," said Tempus handing a letter to the sorcerer who looked worried too.

"If I must I will do fate's will!" said the sorcerer drawing out his sword.

"For stability in the empire, I shall see his will done." swore the sorcerer.

"Who killed fate victim 9 billion 9 hundred and ten?" asked fate of Mortimer, king of the grim reapers.

"We have no record of the killer," said Mortimer.

"Someone has been killing a lot of my victims at late," said fate.

"Yes, and the Fox is worried we have a copycat killer," said Mortimer.

"But he's an insider, not a copycat his victims are from my list," said fate.

"They call him the catch me if you can killer he sent the police a note saying Catch Me If You Can," said Mortimer.

"Enchanter are you the Catch me if you can killer," asked the emperor of the solar system of his son who was fate's former assassin.

"What have I to gain killing for that autocrat again I am on strike," said the Enchanter.

"We think we have an insider killing people of fate's list of people to die for their crimes against-" the emperor was interrupted by his son.

"I know why they die, I am not killing people for fate on the sly," said the Enchanter.

A grim reaper walked into the room.

"Morton, hi," said the Enchanter.

"Hi dad," said the emperor.

"Hi, Blake," said Morton.

"What did you find out," asked Blake.

"I found the killer's name," said Morton looking at the Enchanter nervously.

"Well who is it," asked Blake.

"He did," said Morton pointing at the Enchanter.

"You did? Why? You said you didn't," said Blake horrified.

"Tempus and I were worried you were being corrupted by fate," said the Enchanter coldly glaring at Morton.

"You said you weren't killing for fate," Blake said frowning.

"I was not killing for him, I was killing for you," said the Enchanter.

"How were you killing for me?" asked Blake who looked concerned.

"I wanted to take your place and your guilt as much as I could," said the Enchanter.

"I think you should stop your strike and tell fate who you are," said Morton.

"He's worried we have an insider killing people he wanted them to stop but finding out it was only you, he'll forgive you for doing your job," said Blake.

"Do I have your blessing," asked the Enchanter.

"Do you need it you psychopath," snapped Blake accusingly.

"Thank you," said the Enchanter.

"I'll miss doing Shakespeare," said Blake sadly.

"You old Hamlet!" said the Enchanter.

They all laughed.

Fated to die

"This is different the Necromancer has changed his M O this guy was shot," said a man in a red tux and mask in a top hat standing over a dead body in the street.
"It's not him he's on strike," said a man dressed similarly in blue.
"Then who is the killer?" asked the man in red.
"I don't know, Fox," lied the man in blue.
"Why is he on strike, Enchanter?" asked the Red Fox.
"Who knows shell shock perhaps?" said the Enchanter.
"Shellshock? how he uses a sword?" said the Fox.
Lance didn't want to say a ghost followed the Necromancer home and racked a big power bill to his uncle. He didn't know his secret.
"He may have come to his senses," said Lance.
"Can't see that happening anytime soon," said another masked magician in blue arriving
"Blake, hi, I was trying to figure out who is doing the new Necromancer killings," said the Fox.
"Someone who deserves it!" said Blake.
"You know good, then tell me and we can stop them," said the Fox.
"No they are official deaths the paperwork is done for them and approved. said Blake.
What paperwork?" said the Fox frustration showing in his voice.
"Mortimer himself signed the papers," said Blake who was Mortimer the king of the grim reapers.
"Why would he do that?" asked the Fox.
"Because the killer deserves everything that's coming to him," said Blake.
"Why?" said the Fox.
"He is the one who corrupted the Necromancer," said Blake.
"Fate? Who's he?" asked the Fox.
"Only the Necromancer and Mortimer know. do I look like the grim reaper?" Blake said.
"No, but how do you know so much?" asked the Fox.
"I was briefed by Mortimer," said Blake.
"Oh what did he say," said the Fox.
"The Necromancer was spooked apparently a ghost of a victim followed him home and terrorized his family, so he went on strike," said Blake.
"Terrorized his family, that's enough to make anyone break," said the Fox.
"Sorry got to go a friend needs me," said Blake dematerializing.
"Blake," said Argent otherwise called Fate when Blake rematerialized.
"What?" asked Blake.
"I need you to cover for me again," said Argent.
"Why? More avenging angel work?:" said Blake
"Yes," said Argent who looked shaken by his new job he was shell-shocked from the violence.
"What are you playing?" asked Blake.
"Brutus in Julius Caesar," said Argent.
"Ok, I know the role," said Blake,"am I expected?"
"Yes." said Argent, "they asked for you to take my place the director did Romeo and Juliet. He's a fan of yours."
"No understudy?" asked Blake.
"No, he's sick," said Argent.
"Oh, time and place?" said Blake.
"Now! Here this place," said Argent disappearing,"I got to go! Break a leg!"

Blake's tux melted into a blue and white toga. He walked into the green room.
"Hi all, I'm Marcus Brutus," said Blake.

"I'm Julius Caesar," an actor said, "I'm on, bye, Brutus!"
"Kill you later," said Blake smiling.

All the world's a stage,

"And all the men and women merely players;
They have their exits and their entrances,
And one man in his time plays many parts" said Argent Lumiere in As You Like It by Shakespeare.
"That is true I am playing so many roles for him since he took over Lance's job I sometimes forget
I'm actually a stage magician by profession I feel I am an actor," Blake Alexander said to his wife in
the audience. "You're good honey," his wife replied, "You are just overworking yourself."
He looked at Argent imagining it was him on the stage talking about the many lives the magicians
he knew lived
He was a magician of the stage, he was a superhero, he was the king of the solar system and he was
the king of the reapers of death also a coroner and sometimes an actor, That was just him the others
bore many lives too. He stopped dreaming and his eyes closed.

O Romeo, Romeo! wherefore art thou Romeo?

O Romeo, Romeo! wherefore art thou Romeo?" said Juliet In a production of Shakespeare's Romeo
and Juliet.
Romeo had just dematerialised she was sticking to the script.
"Where did he go?" asked audience member Angela Alexander.
' To do Lance's job I think," said her husband Blake.
"He complained he's being run off his feet doing the Necromancer's killing and paperwork. He has
to run off at odd hours,"
Blake materialised on the stage in the Romeo costume.
"I am Blake Fire will be filling in for Argent as Romeo, He is on pressing business which he
deserves" Blake announced.
"Where did he go?" asked Juliet.
"She speaks:
O, speak again, bright angel! for thou art
As glorious to this night, being o'er my head
As is a winged messenger of heaven" was all Blake said.
The director was livid so she took his lead and they finished the show to great applause. The
director wanted to hire Blake he refused the role saying he wasn't an actor he was an enchanter.

The Threads To Oblivion

"Fate weaves the threads of time till they become the threads of oblivion," said the fate Argent Lumiere to his striking assassin.
"Stop being dramatic you can't convince me to do what you say like that," said the Necromancer.
"Your job is to do my will!" said Argent.
"I'm striking!" said the Necromancer, "it's your turn to be followed home by a demented ghost! He stole my favorite chair and racked up an expensive power bill watching tv all day and night. I tried to get dad to help me get rid of him he just sat down and watched tv with him. No more will I listen to you get off my back monkey!"
"You have to do what I tell you to do!" said Argent shortly
"You won't win!" said the Necromancer, "you can weave time till oblivion comes by yourself for a while!"

The Haunting of the Necromancer

The Necromancer knocked on the door of the office of his father the king of the grim reapers nervously.
"Come in," he heard his father shout back. He walked in the paperwork filled office to see his dad signing and reading papers with a quill and ink.
"Glad to see you give me an excuse to put the pen down. I hate this pen," the Grand Reaper said he looked like a man at that time.
"then why not use a Biro," asked his son.
"Fate says we must use a quill and ink to keep up the Gothic look of the place," said the Grand Reaper, "he likes to have his way as you know."
"Yes," said the Necromancer.
"What brings you to my dingy little office," said the Grand Reaper.
"I wanted to tell you something you should know about," said the Necromancer, "an illegal haunting,"
"I will deal with it," said the Grand Reaper, "tell me about it."

"Well it is in my home," said the Necromancer.
"Your home? how? why?" asked his father.
"One of Fate's chosen to die-" the Necromancer said only to be interrupted by his father.
"The ghost of one of your victims followed you home did they," asked the Grand Reaper.
"Yes, and he's not moving on he's terrorizing my family," said the Necromancer.
"And your children have no powers," said the Grand Reaper, "so it bothers them most,"
"Yes they see their Dad as a dork talking about magic and ghosts being sent to the other side," said the Necromancer.
"Then Granddad will visit and we can get the ghost," said the Grand Reaper.

Later.
There was a knock on the door of the home of the Necromancer.
"Who is it?" asked Lance Alexander.
"Avon calling!" a voice returned.

"Dad?" asked Lance.

"Of course!" grumbled Blake Alexander, "Let me in, boy,"

Lance let him in.

"You ready?" asked Lance.

"I am always ready," Blake said.

"Your Granddad's here children," called Lance's wife.

Out ran Lance's two teenage children.

"Look it's the dork and super dork," said Lance Junior seeing his Dad and Granddad.

"I am not super dork they call me Blue Midnight," said Blake offended,

"and he's The Enchanter we are sorcerers."

"Whatever!" Junior replied.

"You are the biggest fakers magic is not real it is just a trick!" Kristine, Lance's daughter said.

"We are not fake anythings!" said Lance.

"I could debate that with you," said Blake.

"Don't go there in front of my children Dad!" said Lance.

"Where is the ghost?" Blake said changing the subject.

"Him he's watching the TV," said Junior.

"Watching TV?" Blake said skeptically.

"Yeah!" said Kristine.

"What's on is it The Munsters?" asked Blake.

"No, not now that's over he's watching Neighbours," said Junior

"You sure this isn't The Munsters!" Blake asked.

"No! Come with me," Lance said coldly to his dad.

They wandered into the living room the ghost was sitting in Lance's favorite chair watching Neighbours in an eerie scene.

Blake huffed "This is the stupidest haunting I have ever seen! You only want him gone to get your seat back!"

The ghost looked at them.

"Necromancer who's your friend?" the ghost asked.

"He's your worst nightmare," said Lance darkly.

Blake ran into the room and sat on the couch eagerly watching the TV.

"Now I have a ghost and a grim reaper in my lounge room!" said Lance Infuriated.

"A grim reaper where?" asked the ghost in horror.

"Me, the Grand Reaper," said Blake more engrossed in the television than the ghost who he saw as no problem.

"Grand Reaper? What's that?" the ghost asked.

"Another name for a couch potato!" Lance hissed,

"King of the grim reapers, he's meant to get rid of you!"

"Oh, he's no bother, he has good taste! Anyone who likes Neighbours is alright with me" Blake said.

"You watch that tripe!" said Lance.

Blake winked.

"See what I mean!" Blake said.

Then Blake and the ghost laughed.

Lance stood peeked.

"If you won't help I'll get rid of him myself!" shouted Lance his features growing darker.

"Dork why you shouting," said Junior walking in the room.

"Junior! get out of here! Daddy's taking the ghost to the other side!" said Lance.

"Yeah right dork!" said Junior who sat on the couch next to the reaper and watched the show.

"He's in this episode is he," said Junior excitedly seeing an actor in the show.

"Yes, yes this is what I need!" Lance said sarcastically.

Lance walked up to the ghost.

"Get out of the way I can't see the TV!" the ghost complained.

"Get out of his way, boy," Blake hissed.

Lance rolled his eyes.

"You are dead come with me!" said Lance in a voice so funny it made Junior laugh.

"I want to watch this!" said the ghost standing up.

"Quit it stop using the voice let him watch this!" Blake said.

"He is a ghost he shouldn't be watching soapies!" said Lance.

"Dork!" snapped Junior in protest.

After the show finished Lance talked his Dad into letting him take the ghost to the other side.

Lance's children after that called Lance, The Mega Dork.

First Contact

What is that a plane crashing in the park? I better investigate," thought Blake Alexander seeing a strange light in the sky.

It turned out to be a UFO landing.

"Oh an x-zeracian ship," said Blake recognizing it.

"Should be neighborly and see what they want. "

"Take us to your leader," the grey alien said,

"I am my leader, the emperor of this system," said Blake, "what brings you to my system."

"We want to make our presence known," the alien said.

"You are known I've seen you're people before I'm descended from your race," Blake said.

"Oh," said the alien, " then we'll go."

Then they left again. Sad and dejected they wanted make first contact and they met one of the descendants of their race so they weren't first.

It wasn't the end of this Blake was chased for months later by the men in black till they realized he was not going to be a problem as he was an alien like the men in black and the x-zerracians so it was merely an alien meeting aliens.

Lend me your ears

Friends, Romans, countrymen, lend me your ears;

I come to bury Caesar, not to praise him." said Argent Lumiere who was Playing Marc Antony in a production of Julius Caesar.

A man walked from the auditorium on stage dropping a pile of ears out of an old wooden bucket at Argent's feet.

"Mind I'm only lending them," said the Necromancer obviously amused.

"And I must pause till it come back to me." said the infuriated actor trying to get back in character.

The audience thought it was a joke they were in stitches.

"I can't believe it!" Angela Alexander said in disbelief.

"I can he took those ears from his victims,' said her husband darkly.

"They are real ears?" asked Angela nervously.

"with him, they would be he is telling Argent he's going on strike," Blake Alexander said, " I spoke to Lance about his striking earlier today but, I didn't expect this."

The Magicians : To be or not to be

To be, or not to be: that is the question: Whether 'tis nobler in the mind to suffer The slings and arrows of outrageous fortune, Or to take arms against a sea of troubles, And by opposing end them?" said Hamlet on the stage played by fate Argent Lumiere.

"Argent was well cast," a lady in the audience whispered to her husband.

"Yes Hamlet is his dream job," Blake Alexander whispered back to her.

"He's very good," said Angela his wife.

"What do you expect from a fate like him he takes his job too seriously," Blake said.

"I have some paperwork for you, Blake," Argent said in their heads he had apparently had been eavesdropping.

It rained paperwork on Blake's head.

"Darn more paperwork," Blake moaned.

Dark Star

You remember this guy don't you," said the Red Fox slapping the back of a masked magician in a black tux.

"Is he the masked magician?" asked a policeman who was new to the area so had no Idea who this was.

"I never reveal tricks!" the man in black said.

"No he's my nephew Dark Star, " said the Fox.

"Oh, ok one of you!" said the policeman.

"He's going to help on our case," said the Fox.

"I thought the Enchanter and Blue midnight were helping on the case do we need more help," said the policeman.

"Hi dad," Blue Midnight said seeing Dark Star.

"Hi Midnight where is Enchanter I heard he was hereabouts," said Dark Star.

"He's with Astra they are talking to the victim," said Blue Midnight.

"How can they do that he was murdered!" said the police man.

"My great-granddaughter Astra is a medium," said Dark Star.

"I don't believe in them," huffed the policeman.

"And still she is a medium," said Blue Midnight laughing.

"Let's join them there," said the Fox and they went to just Astra and the Enchanter.

"Hello dad, gramps," said the Enchanter seeing them.

Astra was under.

"Who?" she asked.

"Oh sorry. wasn't talking to you," the Enchanter said to the ghost,

"Excuse me guys," he said to the newcomers.

"Who killed you?" the Enchanter asked the ghost.

"How should I know I'm dead!" said Astra.

"Any clues?" asked the Enchanter.

"Yes I heard a bang then I was dead," said Astra.

"Oh, that's what he said in his debrief to Mortimer," Blue Midnight said.

"Who is Mortimer," asked the policeman.

"The king of the grim reapers," said Blue Midnight.

"king of the what- you've got to be joking," the policeman laughed.

"No joke he's a pain in the neck and he has a paperwork fetish," the Enchanter said.

"He has not," snapped Blue Midnight.

"He's real I met him," said Astra who was still under.

"Me too," the Enchanter, " he's a skeleton in a black monks outfit."

"He's son is the Necromancer a serial killer he's fate's hit-man," said Blue Midnight.

"Fate who that a gangster?" the policeman asked.

"You are new to town," said the Enchanter.

"Fate is Fate," said the Fox.

"So all we know is the victim was shot." Dark Star said sadly,

"What did he do?"

" He was a criminal lawyer," said Lance, "no lose there from what I've heard of him he deserved to die."

"No one deserves to die," said Blue Midnight coldly.

"You haven't met some of the people who I have," said the Enchanter,

"I met them," Blue Midnight said glaring at his son.

"There is nothing wrong with lawyers my wife is a lawyer," said Dark Star.

"I understand but he got off murderers," said the Enchanter.

"Everyone deserves a chance in law," said Dark Star,

"Maybe," said the Enchanter.

"I think we need to meet the suspect in casual clothes so they don't realise who we are?" said Dark Star.

"Good idea," Blue Midnight said they were known to the police.

Days later.

"We have you here as suspects in the murder of Charles Vincent," said the police sergeant Simon Xander-Drax.

"Who are they?" asked the wife of the victim.

"Observers," said Simon,

"I know who he is I saw his show last night!" said the brother of the victim.

All of the observers stood stony-faced but nervous inside.

"That's Blake Fire," said the brother.

"Good evening," Blake said.

"Can I have an autograph?" the brother asked.

"Ok," Blake said pulling out a card with his autograph on.

"Why are you here?" asked the brother.

"I was curious what uncle Simon did as a job so were they we want to observe him at work," said Blake.

"Who are they," asked the wife.

"Friends," Blake said.

"what are their names?" asked the wife.

"Valentine," one man said.

"Astra," the woman observer said.

"Lance," another male said.

"Uncle Sie you do your work we are just here to watch you work," Blake said to his great-uncle.

"Yes," said Valentine.

"You are the suspect in the murder of Charles Vincent," Simon said.

"I did do it," said the wife, nor did I another person said.

"I killed him but no one can prove it," a voice among many rang in the heads of Lance, Valentine Astra, Blake, and Simon.

"Did you hear that the killer was thinking he was home free he confessed in his mind," said Blake in the mind of Simon and the other observers.

"We heard," thought Lance.

"We need to get them alone too many voices to pin them," thought Astra.

"We will need you talk to every one alone," Simon said.

"Ok," the wife said.

"Can we observe?" asked Blake who seemed to be the leader of the observers.

"Of course, Blake you can see how I work," said Simon.

Later.

"Last suspect no clues yet," said Lance to Blake. before the last suspect entered the room.

"Yes," Blake said, "the killer is sloppy he thinks we can't read his mind."

" Uncle Simon is bringing in the last suspect quiet, " said Valentine.

Then in walked Simon with a woman from the crowd of suspects.

"Who is she?" asked Astra.

"The mistress of the victim," Simon said.

"Mistress- oh?" said Astra.

"Sit down my dear," Simon said.

The mistress sat and Simon started recording.

"I am Senior Sergeant Simon Xander-Drax I am interviewing Kelly Drake the mistress of the victim," Simon said,

"Observing are Lance, Blake and Valentine Alexander and Astra Demarney-Gray,"

"Are you all related," asked Kelly.

"Yes," Lance said.

"cousins," Kelly asked.

"Something like that," said Blake not wanting to admit their true relationships as it would be as good as admitting who they were.

"Where were you when Charles Vincent was murdered," asked Simon.

"I was at home," Kelly said.

"I know that was a bad alibi but what else could I say I was there killing him," rang into the heads of the Enchanter: Lance, Blue Midnight: Blake, Dark Star: Valentine, the Red Fox: Simon and Astra.

"Another Confession," said Blake.

"What," asked Kelly "I said I was at home I know it's a bad alibi I made no confessions this is entrapment."

"We are mind readers," Lance said.

"Sergeant," said Kelly looking for a little sympathy and sensibility/

"So am I we all heard you confess!" Simon said.

"We are sorcerers and a sorceress," said Valentine.

"Astra and a grim reaper spoke to Mr Vincent's ghost we had no clues. So we rounded up the suspect in order to read their minds in case we could get a confession mentally where heard you confess before and again thus," said Simon.

"Why did you kill him?" asked Blake.

"He threatened to leave me," Kelly said.

"Why were you armed in Australia it's illegal to carry arms," said Simon.

"I carried it to threaten him not kill him he said he'd leave me so I shot him," said Kelly.

"The old If I can't have him no one can excuse is it?" said Simon.

"Yes," Kelly said.

Thus the case was solved and they had witnesses to the confession.

The Masked Chicken

The Mask Chicken is a hero,
his saves run to zero,
he's actually a serial pest,
even if he does his best,
he gets in the the way,
he never saves the day

The Magicians: The Haunting of Death-Extended

I am beyond life,
I am beyond strife,
I am long beyond my last breath,
I'm among the angelic host,
some call me a ghost,

I awoke one day dead or as good as dead,
I knew not how it was even possible me being a ghost
as I was the king of the grim reapers, so I cannot die in a normal way as this to become a ghost.

I was not dead, I was not alive I was somewhere in between in a strange unknown limbo.

strange as it did seem. I awoke in my home
and found that there I did roam
til the necromancer saw me and asked me what was wrong.
I hadn't been at work in days know no one knew because my plight because my wife was away.
He was a reaper he did try help.
I worked as the grand reaper doing my paperwork from home and Lance filled in on the stage until
one day I came back to life.
The day my wife came back. I blame fate for that ever the prankster he was he dare not keep up the
prank with my wife his cousin there.

Tales from the Crypt

I once met a man from an old land,
who told me of the creatures of the night please understand,
he was a hunter by trade,

before me a bloody wooden stake he laid,

he muttered the blood is the life,
looking at it I wonder why not use a knife,
I asked what he did hunt with a stake,
he said vampires before they wake,

he used the stake I had no doubt,
I said the dead do not go out,
he knew I did not believe
so he did apologize and took his leave.

Blind Faith

"I hate murderers!" said the downtrodden coroner called by his hospital colleagues Dr. Death. In truth most didn't know his actual name, all but his wife Dr. Angela Alexander. She was his assistant. "Blake this is the 7th magician to die here I think it is more than just a person killing at random," Angela said. "I know they were more than magicians. They were sorcerers, Angel," Blake said, "not human it seems someone has a grudge here." "That's why I'm here!" said Lance, Blake's son. "What can you do kill more people?" Angela asked. "No I am bate!" said Lance. "Yes, he will be hard to kill," Blake said. "You can't use our son as bate," Angela said gruffly. "I volunteered to be bate and he can't stop me I'd be here if he said no too!" Lance said. "Never could stop him doing anything even murder!" Blake said. "I am to be a sick sorcerer patient who prefers magic to manual labor," Lance said. "To draw out the killer," Blake said. "I still don't like the idea," Angela said, "I'll be near by shout if you need help." Later... "Stop whining or I'll silence you myself," Lance said in a hospital bed next to a man in pain who had been moaning a lot. "Shut up you," a grumpy male nurse shouted at Lance. "He's in pain not sure why you are here," "I was put here because I'm insane," Lance said. "Really what did you do?" the nurse asked. "I pulled a hat out of a rabbit!" said Lance. "how did the rabbit take it!" asked the nurse. "It died," said Lance sadly. "You are mad!" said the nurse. As Lance sat pulling air out of cards as only a sorcerer could. The nurse looked at Lance's clipboard and looked worried. "I'm worse than that says," said Lance laughing darkly. "Mr. Silver," said Lance's doctor walking in the room. "how have you been?" "Bored as hell and my neighbour is a pain," said Lance. "What are you doing?" the doctor asked. "Pulling air out of cards, any fake can pull cards out of the air," Lance said laughing. "You are an insane lunatic!" said the doctor whacking his head in frustration. "You leave your neighbor alone. He has a kidney stone," The doctor straightened his glasses which weren't slipping. "I don't want any more paperwork," Blake snapped at his patient. "You and paperwork!" said Lance. Then it started raining paperwork over Blake's head. Lance saw his father biting his lip to not speak. Lance got up and touched the kidney stone victim. "You say this guy has a kidney stone I say he hasn't!" said Lance. Blake was livid. "Stop healing my patients!" snapped Blake who snapped his fingers returning the stone to the patient. "Whatever you say, doc!" said Lance, "want me to make them sick?" "No just no walking on water or curing cripples and raising the dead on my watch thank you!" said Blake. "Sacrilege!" the nurse cried in horror. "Are you alright?" Lance asked. "You can't do what he said! The Lord is the only one who can," said the nurse. "I'll only walk on puddles, cure boredom and raise cards ok?" Lance said. "He's got a messiah complex. But I can assure you he's not the messiah as they say on The Life of Bryan 'He's not the messiah he's a very naughty boy'" Blake said. "Oh! really then who thinks he's the angel of death?" Lance who couldn't take the insult retorted. Blake snarled under his breath. "Dr. Death not the angel of death!" Blake snapped, "you are as useful as a blunt knife!" "Honey stop arguing with the patients!" Angela said running into the room hearing the argument from outside the room. "He cured my patient." Blake complained, "I had to make him sick again he dies in his operation tonight." "You are one of him?" said the nurse. "Not quite!" said Blake, "I'm an emperor he's just a madman," "Madman! I'm rabid, Dad," said Lance, "he's our man!" "I know boy I read minds too!" Blake said, "He was planning to murder you." "Nobody murders the Necromancer," said Lance, "I'd kill them!" "Not this one boy, we throw this one to the laws of man," Blake said, "No divine justice here! He wants to kill us because he thinks witches are sacrilegious abominations. He sees himself as a witch hunter killing us for his faith!" "But he knows who I am," said Lance, "Not when I've finished with him!" Blake said darkly. "Is he dying?" asked Lance. "Nothing of the sort! I will hypnotize him he's going to sing about what he did but forget us. You got your powers of enchantment from me. Enchanter or did you forget?" Blake said. Later... Blake lay dead on a slab in the morgue. As a strange hooded creature crept about the hospital looking for the dead. He walked into an operating room. "Come with me you died of complications of the operation." the grim reaper hissed, "I'll have to tell your family later and I'll have more paperwork!"

A vampire love poem : Extended

It was her chaos that made her beautiful,
her heart that made me love her,
her love that made me live even beyond my heart's stopping beating.

I am dead to you maybe but I am also dead to me : extended

Yes, I survived the car accident, but that is only because I was already long dead, I live yet I do not live so I survived death in death

What's done cannot be undone

What is done cain't be undone," said a Macbeth actor in the performance of the show. The audience laught at him.
"He got it wrong again!" The director of the show said to Argent Lumiere an actor was in the show and just happened to be a fate.
"why did you give him the role," said argent,
"He's a big actor in America," said the director.
"The south?" asked Argent.
"Yes," said the director,
"You got him for his name I suppose," Argent said,

"Yes," said the director,

"I told you, you to cast me in the role," said Argent.

"I wish I did," the director said, "anyone would be better than him."

In the audience, a man in a tux said to his new wife.

"This is bad for Argent, Angela,"

"Blake how.is it bad for him,"Angela, his wife asked.

"He's doing it to the man," Blake Alexander said.

"how? why?" his wife asked.

"He wanted the role so he is manipulating the man, into acting bad and mispronouncing his lines and getting everything wrong, he's a fate he can do that and he's a sore loser, I know. He turned me into a grim reaper because he was," said Blake.

Fall out

Apparently the man was killed because he knew too much and was going to speak in court so someone silenced him!" a grim reaper said matter of factly to the sergeant of police in a rather odd looking scene that of a morgue.

"Mortimer who killed him?" asked the sergeant in no way scared or nervous talking to him seemed natural.

"The ghost did not say, he said he knew nothing of the crime he was going to reveal or his own death! I take it as a 3 wise monkeys case!" said Mortimer matter of factly.

"You mean he won't say what he knows!" said Reynard Alexander the sergeant.

"Yes!" Spoke the reaper in a dying voice,"What was he going to tell the court?"

"The true identity of-" Reynard was interrupted by the entrance a man in blue tux top hat and mask he looked nervous.

"Lancelot Alexander!" scoffed Reynard who was his grandfather's and mother's uncle. His parents were cousins, "Why are you nervous around our friend Mortimer!"

"There must be another reason," snarled the reaper who knew Lance was hiding some dark secrets. "This is probably the work of the Necromancer," Mortimer hissed.

"I wouldn't know?" said Lance off-handedly, "If it was him the man deserved it."

"I have no doubt the Necromancer thinks so," said the reaper.

"Uncle where is my father something has happened," said Lance looking the reaper dead in the eyes.

"What has happened that you need him?" asked the reaper.

"I haven't seen him today," said Reynard.

"Mother is in hospital," said Lance nervously.

Reynard was speechless he loved her she was his niece and he hadn't heard of it. He and his brothers had arranged their marriage at first Blake and she despised each other. Later they grew to love each other deeply. Blake was the heir to the empire of the solar system. He was now emperor. She was the daughter of the king of time. They saw great promise in the match she was called the angel of time, their powers were inherited by one of their sons The Timekeeper, the most powerful being of their race and the most lonely but enough of him.

"Why didn't you tell us before you psycho!" said the reaper his voice no longer disguised it was Blake who spoke.

"She was attacked in a home invasion she's critical! She was shot and the doctors are worried she won't make the night," Lance said not wanting to be the one to tell the reaper his wife was dying.

"I had better go find, friend Blake," said Mortimer in his disguised voice.

"Me too!" Lance said dematerializing after his father.

A man in a Doctor's outfit came dashing out of a medicines cupboard in the Hospital.

"There you are Doctor, we were looking everywhere for you. We have another job for you," an orderly said.

"For heaven's sake don't beat around the bush!" Grumbled the Doctor.

"Another freshy for you!" said the orderly.

"Please refrain from referring to them as freshies call them a dead person!" hissed the doctor.

"Ok another dead person!" said the orderly.

"Take me to them," the doctor demanded.

"Doctor Death has come to do his job announced the orderly to the nervous nurse inside the room with the body.

"I'm a coroner, not Doctor Death," said the Doctor entering the room.

"So sorry!" a reaper said walking out of the room. The doctor ran to the bedside of the dead person.

"Oh my god no," the doctor said weeping tears of blue electric fire which crystalized betraying his inhumanity to his colleagues.

"Blue Midnight is Doctor Death!" cried the orderly.

"Really Sherlock how didn't you know!" said Blake crying,

"I was called here by my son because my wife was critical!"

"I just told him about his wife's death! Hey! That's your job telling people their relatives are dead!" the orderly moaned.

"I'll do you the same favor one day!" snarled Blake.

"Who killed her?" roared Blake.

"We don't know!" the nurse said.

"I will not rest till she is avenged!" screamed Blake.

"Now you are talking like me," Lance said entering the room.

Blake embraced the man he despised most in the world his own son, who he saw as a monster. He was also known as the Necromancer, Fate's avenger or to Blake a mad violent serial killer lead by the nose by his boss the last Fate, Argent, who was Mortimer's boss too but Blake never liked or trusted him. Argent had turned the young dashing, heroic, Emperor into the king of the grim reapers nothing to make him trust him. Lance had his father's powers of sorcery and Necromancy. Like his long-dead sister had.

"If he's Blue Midnight then you are his son the Enchanter!" the nurse

said in awe of them they were alien superheroes to the world. Their darker lives were less well known.

"I'll help you," said Lance coldly, "no one escapes my vengeance!"

"For god's sake stop boasting you psycho! your mother lies freshly murdered," Blake snapped.

"Stop fighting you two enter the vortex I need you!" a crying voice shouted from a swirling vortex.

They walked into it, a man in tears greeted them.

Blake hugged him.

"Son," said Blake crying.

"I can't help save Mum, but we can avenge her," said the man, "in the past I saw him!"

"In the pool of time," said Lance.

"Come," said the man leading them to a glowing pool of water with the attack repeating in it. they heard him speak as he shot her "A life for a life!" he said and he shot her and it repeated.

"This him?" asked Blake seeing a man he knew.

"Yes, you met him the dead stool pigeon," said the man.

"Him? then maybe I did murder him after all," Lance said.

"Was he blackmailing Lance?" Blake asked.

"No, Dad was being blackmailed or will be when you go back!" said the man.

"Why?" Blake asked.

"He finds out you are Mortimer and he wants you sent to prison as a murderer!" said the man.

"I didn't kill anyone!" said Blake.

"Mortimer took his wife," the man said.

"She died I took her for processing," said Blake.

"He doesn't see it that way," said the man.

"How did she die?" Lance asked.

"You killed her, Lance," Blake lied. Lance felt terrible thinking he caused his own mother's death.

"She was in a car accident!" said Blake seriously.

Lance scowled.

"How did he die?" Lance asked.

"I will attack him with my sword, the sword of time," said the man, "to protect my family."

"Tempus, The Timekeeper! You never leave the tunnels of time for any reason let alone to murder a man!" Lance said shocked.

"I saw it so it will happen," Tempus said.

"No wonder the killer of your Mum's ghost is refusing to talk!" Blake said, "He doesn't want to help or antagonize us more!"

"Is there any chance of saving Mum?" asked Lance

"No, but she will be avenged!" Tempus said.

"When are we going to?" Blake asked.

"2 days before you left!" Tempus said, "don't let your younger selves see you."

"Why?" Lance said.

"You don't know you are there! Don't want to change the past much!" Tempus said.

"We saved the moon from a space cuckoo why can't we save our Mum?" Lance asked, "can we save her by not going back to save her?"

"This is a fixed point in time! You can't go back it has already happened. The moon wasn't a fixed point and it was the Moon. Without it, there is no Earth! you were saving the Earth!" Tempus said. "Enter the vortex and do what already happened."

"Here we go again," said Lance as they walked in the vortex.

Fate digs up a friend

A man in a mask and a tux stood by a grave of his friend's dead wife.

"Angela Alexander you will live again!" The man said, "You will reincarnate in the past!"

"Argent. What are you doing lurking in the graveyard!" Angela's grieving widower snapped finding it an odd place to find fate.

"Oh hi, Mortimer what bring the king of the grim reapers here?" Argent said.

"My wife is buried here It gives me a right and reason to be here," said the reaper Mortimer.

"Isn't she in your realm?" asked Argent.

"Only her soul, not seen her since she was processed," Mortimer said,

"Oh shame," said Argent, "no job perks."

"No, reapers are not meant to see their wives and families after death rule-" Mortimer was interrupted.

"Quit with the paperwork she's your wife!" Argent snapped.

"I know a lady you may like," Argent said leading Mortimer from his wife grave.

"There can never be anyone for me but Angela you busybody," said the reaper.

"We'll see!" said Argent smiling.

"What are you up too?" said Mortimer.

"You'll see!" said Argent.

A woman woke up with all the memories of Angela one day.

"What dream!" she said to her self, "I feel like new person."

"This is my cousin," said Argent to Blake Alexander a downtrodden mocked Doctor at Queenscross hospital.

"Wait a second you don't have any cousins let alone relatives!" said Blake seeing a trap.

"No I do, shes new to the area can you show her around," said Argent.

"You are the last fate! Since when were their two?" said Blake."You're trying to play cupid It won't work!"

"No, I'm not she's working at your hospital her first day this is!" said Argent.

"Oh good day dear lady!" said Blake politely.

"Hi Blake I'm Angela I'm back," said the woman.

"I see Dr. Angela Silver," said Blake reading her name tag.

"No, I'm Angela!" said the woman frustrated.

"Ok Angela it is then," said Blake.

"No I am Angela Alexander!" said Angela.

"No you are not my wife she's dead!" said Blake, "Or should be! Argent have you trained her to say that she's my wife I won't have her! But I'll help her! Whoever she is!"

"Good, all I wanted," lied Argent,

"Careful girl he thinks you are someone else and not his wife reincarnated!" said Argent in her mind.

"Well I work here rather dead at the moment," he said trying to break the ice.

"Oh it's a morgue!" she said laughing.

"I work here too I was assigned as your assistant," said Angela,

"Well nobody told me! No one notices me except when some on dies then it's time to drag Dr. Death out of the morgue!" said Blake frustrated

"Ok this is the slab!" said Blake pointing, "The freezers are out there so is my office"

"Can I see your office!" she asked.

"Ok," Blake said it was a dark dingy room full of paperwork on the wall she saw a poster it read "Cold Play" and "Death and all his friends"

Angela laughed she knew who he was.

"A joke?" Angela asked.

"What?" asked Blake.

"The poster!" she said.

"No I like Cold Play good album that one!" said Blake.

"Oh!" said Angela,"Me too!"

Angela pulled out her phone and looked for it in her music all she could find there was the phantom of the opera song from the movie.

"It's not there," she said.

"what?" said Blake.

"Cold Play song 42, I thought I had it here all I have I phantom of the opera!" she said.

"Sounds like Argent's in your mind," Blake laughed.

"What do you mean?" asked Angela.

"He plays with people like puppets," said Blake.

"But I had it on my phone," said Angela.

"No my wife did she loved it," Blake said smiling remembering her.

"Oh!" said Angela.

"I'll play it for you!" Blake said pulling out his phone.

"Those who are dead are not dead they are in my mind," Angela sang along with the band.

"My Angel used to love singing along with the album," said Blake.

"Did she," asked Angela realizing whose phone it was that had the song on.

All of the dead bodies in the morgue screamed at once.

"What's wrong?" Angela asked.

"I have to go to work a soul is missing in the underworld," said Blake.

"Is that what it means?" asked Angela.

"No a reaper just told me that was just to get my attention," Blake said.

"Dad she likes you," said the reaper.

"I know Necromancer she is suspicious," Blake said in the Reaper's mind "She's crazy too she thinks she's your Mum."

"She maybe she's the one missing!" said their son.

"Argent!" screamed Blake.

"What do you want, Blake?" Argent snapped appearing he looked like cupid a bit,

"What are you wearing!" Blake asked.

"I'm an actor in costume I just left the stage I was playing Puck!" said Argent.

"Oh you are a fairy!" Blake said, "I thought you were playing Cupid!"

"No!" said Argent.

"I still am not convinced you aren't!" said Blake,"What have you done with my wife's soul?"

"Nothing!" said Argent.

"Then why did you sign for it?" Blake snapped.

"I signed for, what?" Argent asked.

"The magic which took her from Elysian was yours," accused Blake.

"I reincarnated her!" said Argent.

"You mean she's my wife?" Blake asked looking at Angela.

"I told you I was!" said Angela, "what is Lance doing here?"

"You see me?" her son said nervously.

"Of course always could!" said Angela "stop the screamers I can't think." The dead went quiet.

"How dare you mess with this poor woman and my wife's soul!" said Blake.

"How dare I save her life I made this woman to carry your wife's soul she is my cousin!" said Argent, "I did this for you and her!"

"Now what do we do," asked Blake. Angela kissed him.

"I am your wife we live happily ever after again," Angela said.

Blake stood dumbstruck not sure what to do or say.

"We'll be fine," said Angela.

"I told you that you would like her!" said Argent.

"Angel I don't know what to do? I can't kill you for your soul!" Blake said,

"I'll have to get used to this!" He kissed her back.

Dark side of the moon

The grim reaper sat drinking a cup of coffee as a man in his office peacefully until his son ran in his office. "Dad you won't believe it the moon has hatched!" The Necromancer shouted. His father choked on his coffee.

"You alright Dad?" asked Lance worried.

"Yes, you psycho! The moon did what?" Blake, his dad said to his serial killer son.

"This is more important than you and me! The moon has hatched It was an egg!" Lance said hardly believing it himself and he saw it with his own eyes.

"Ok, I'll try to prioritize! What came out a mega space chicken?" asked Blake who was also the emperor of the solar system.

"If only it was a space chicken!" Lance said sadly.

"Then what hatched from it?" Ask his father.

"A giant space locust!" said Lance.

"Oh no they are world killers, they are worse than you!" said Blake,"They lay eggs in planets!" said Blake standing.

"Dad I am fate's-" Lance moaned.

"Assassin!" Blake interrupted.

"Whatever! We have a solar system to protect!" said Lance.

" Ok, then come on boy we need to get help," Blake said.

They ran out of the office. Through the gates of the other world and into the dimensional portal leading to the Earth and appeared in Blake's backyard. They paused slightly seeing the locust!

"Oh my God!" Blake said seeing the giant planet killer. It resembled a praying mantis. "It looks like fate wonder if they're related?" Lance said.

"Wouldn't surprise me he's insane, sending you off to kill people he doesn't like!" Blake said "I've not seen a space locust before," Blake stood in awe of the beast.

"How do we kill it before it kills another planet!" asked Lance.

"I don't have a clue how we can stop It!" The Emperor said, "Send fate to have a pow-wow with it?" A portal opened in front of them.

"Enter the portal, please!" A voice said emitting from the portal said.

"Come on boy," Blake said walking in first.

on the other side was a man who resembled them who was sitting by a glowing pool of water with images appearing in its crystalline waters.

"Tempus how you been," Lance said to the man.

"Better than the moon!," Tempus said.

"Hi boy, what do you want?" Blake said putting his hand on Tempus's shoulder.

"Hi dad, I know how to kill it but the Earth needs the moon!" said Tempus.

"What can we do?" asked Blake, "Should I sic Lance on it?"

"Dad!" Lance said embarrassed and angry at the comment.

"Yes, the job will need you too! It can only be done in the past!" said Tempus, "when the moon was implanted!"

"How do you kill them?" Lance asked.

"Get Lance to do it!" Blake said shortly, "He's good at killing!"

"They are Allergic to the fire of suns!" said Tempus ignoring the comment.

"Starfire!" said Blake, "can do! We have some ancestors from the sun! Just blast it and it's gone right?"

"Yes!" Tempus said.

"Send us to the time when the egg was laid," said Blake.

"The portal over there," said Tempus pointing at it.

"Ok here we go," Lance said as they entered the portal.

They appeared on the moon thirty million years before.

Had they been 5 minutes earlier they would have seen the mother locust injecting its egg into the moon All they saw was the mother she was bigger than her child the egg was hidden.

"She's really big!" Lance thought when they arrived.

"Stop admiring her we have to kill her! You know how too kill don't you!" Blake said reading his mind.

"Not going there! You can take it to hell with you!" Lance grumbled in his mind.

The reaper snarled.

They walked towards it when it saw them they were like fleas.

it tried to squash them. It missed. It tried again to swipe them and near skewered Blake. Lance saved him by making him disappear and reappear somewhere else. "Now!" Blake said in his mind and they released the power of the sun on the locust. It blew up.

"She's dead!" Lance thought.

"I think your right!" Blake thought.

Back to the portal, they went.

"It was easier than I thought!" said Lance.

"It was, you have to go back!" Tempus said.

"What?" Lance said.

"The moon still hatched you missed the egg," said Tempus.

"Oh!" said Lance.

Back on the moon minutes later thirty million years earlier.

"We need to cleanse the moon," Blake thought " with a solar storm!"

They created one a mega-storm there was an explosion.

"Got it!" Blake said in Lance's head, "Thanks for saving me before! Let's go back!"

"You are welcome!" Lance thought."Yes, let's go! The moon is nice only from a distance! I wonder how our ancestors lived here!"

"You got it," said Tempus, the timekeeper when they got back, "You can go home now!"

"Bye son," Blake said hugging his son Tempus.

"Bye father and brother, don't kill each other!" said Tempus.

Lance laughed and said, "See you around!" and they walked in a portal and were gone.

I bear the wounds of all the battles I avoided

My parents were murdered when I was very young around the time I became a vampire. I was raised by my uncle Lance he was a very good father. I am a sorceress and a werewolf a daywalker vampire and the queen of the vampires.

"This is Astra Starfire, my niece, She's the wife of Max Starfire the noted stage Magician," uncle Lance said we were at a crime scene.

Apparently, someone had been murdered by a vampire and I was a vampire expert and I was a necromancer so I could talk to the dead.

"Hello Astra, " the detective in charge of the case said,"how's Max not seen him for a while!" Max also helped out the police.

"He's cleaning the town on public service still after his car accident," I said in reply.

"I am sorry to hear that," said the detective," but his passenger did die."

"Yes," I said, but so would have my husband if he wasn't already a vampire.

"I am here to talk to the victim," I said.

"Yes," my uncle Lance said. I got myself ready to be possessed.

"Ready?" asked my uncle.

"Yes," I said and touched the hand of the victim who was on a slab covered by a sheet their hand was uncovered.

I felt myself going under.

"What is going on where am I?" I heard myself saying. I felt disoriented like I was lost.

"My niece is acting as a medium you are in her to tell us how you died and who killed you?" uncle Lance said.

"I don't believe in mediums!" I heard myself say.

"Maybe so but she is acting as one," uncle Lance said laughing. Then he was serious his eyes grew cold his voice commanding I know that look and voice he was using necromancy to control the ghost.

"Tell us of the last moments of your life!" my uncle said.

"I was bitten on the neck then I died," I heard myself say I felt compelled to speak it wasn't me it was the ghost I sense.

"Five minutes before you died," said my uncle in the same voice.

"I was dancing at a masquerade with Ellen Michaels my killer," I heard myself say I felt angry or the ghost did, me personally I was panicking inside me I realized he was my victim I pushed the ghost out of me.

"Astra is anything wrong?" asked my uncle.

"I can't be here!" I said in his head and disappeared into thin air.

I bear the wounds of all the battles I've avoided.

I felt I have a close brush with another such battle.

"You were the killer I take it," uncle Lance said later.

"I'm afraid I was! I gave a false name in case someone asked about me," I said.

"I'm sorry to involve you in this," he said.

"What happened after I left?" I asked him.

"I lied said you were ill," said my uncle, "I reported the ghost was being unreasonable and was most likely given a false name so his evidence would not be accurate."

"Thanks," I said.

"You are my family? My family is worth protecting," said my Uncle.

You can't kill a skeleton with a knife

Darn more paperwork!" moaned a man in a blue top hat and tux in a mask. He was known as Blue Midnight, a superhero. His son hit him on the back and laughed. "You love paperwork what are you worried about," said his son laughing.

"Get out of my hair boy," Blake snapped at his son Lance who was dress similarly in blue.

"You'd think you didn't love me," said his son sarcastically.

"Not now I'm on a case Enchanter," Blake then said accusingly "The Necromancer Murdered another person."

"Oh that is terrible! Did I know them?" Lance asked.

"You tell me! We can't id them. We are going to have to do DNA tests and tooth tests, not much left of them," Blake said disgustedly.

"That bad eh!" Lance said sadly.

"That's not the only one, he struck again yesterday," Blake said.

Lance lost the sarcastic manner he had. He looked shocked.

"The other murder wasn't him someone framed him! He's innocent as a lamb," Lance said.

"I could never call him a lamb, he's a wolf," Blake said.

"Who was framed," a man in a red Tux, mask and top hat said walking up to them.

"Hi! Fox, he thinks someone framed the Necromancer," said Blake, "still the same to me more paperwork!"

"We have to investigate whoever the killer is!" Reynard, the Red Fox said.

"True," Lance said, "it's starting to look like anyone can kill people!"

"If you aren't going to help us then go away you psycho!" Blake said who knew the Necromancer was Lance.

"But, he's been framed!" Lance said.

"Why do you care? He's a murderer!" said Reynard, he didn't know Lance's secret, "how do you know he's innocent anyway?"

"He was with me yesterday!" said Lance grabbing for an alibi.

"You were with him?" said the Fox sceptically.

"Yes!" Lance said desperately.

"When and why!" asked the Fox.

"All day!" said Lance not knowing when the other victim died.

"All day! You spent the day with him! An insane murdering killer?" said the Fox.

"He is- my- err," said Lance who was having a hard time thinking.

"He's Lance's better half!" Blake said frowning.

"He's your boyfriend," shouted the Fox Insanely. Lance's eyes widened.

"Is there something wrong with that!" Lance snapped glaring at Blake he wasn't having an affair with anyone but his wife let alone himself.

"He's an insane, violent serial killer!" the Fox shouted.

"He'd never hurt me," Lance said telling the truth.

"Who is he?" asked the Fox.

"Search me?" Lance said, "I don't know!"

"Mind If I go, Uncle Rey, I want to clear my name! err my partner's name!" Lance said trying to get away.

"No you stay!" said Reynard grabbing his wrist, "why are you and your father blocking your minds."

"We aren't!" Blake said defensively.

"Now, why would we do that?" said Lance thinking he couldn't go much lower without coming out as the Necromancer he'd already come out as a cheating partner and gay when he was neither.

"You know something! Both of you do!" Reynard hissed.

"My thoughts are private!" Lance protested he pulled his arm free and stomped off.

"What is he hiding Blake you know?" Reynard, the sergeant snapped.

In reply, Blake disappeared into thin air. Leaving Reynard alone and frustrated.

"Morton, please follow Lance," Blake ordered a grim reaper.

"Why?" asked the reaper.

"He may need help I suspect he may have been framed, he's in trouble more than usual!" Blake said,

"Don't let him see you,"

"Ok, Blake," Morton said to his son.

"Send the ghost in the foyer in when you leave, Dad," Blake said.

Morton walked out of the dingy paperwork littered office of Blake.

"Why am I here?" the ghost asked.

"You were murdered!" Blake said.

"I know!" said the ghost, "But, what are you doing here you aren't dead!"

"Don't hold that against me! I am on your case! I'm the coroner in charge of your case!" said Blake.

"What is a coroner doing in the afterlife," said the ghost.

"I'm not going there," Blake said, "I want to know who killed you!"

"I saw a man I don't know in blue jeans and a red parker!" the ghost said. Blake pulled out a picture out of a folder on his bench. It was a picture of Lance in masked in a black outfit holding a sword obviously taken by a reaper without Lance knowing,

"Is he anyone special?" asked the ghost seeing it.

"He is Fate's Hand of Justice or so he thinks, he's actually Fate's assassin!" Blake said.

"Is he your brother he looks a lot like you!" said the ghost.

"He's my son, not my brother," Blake said.

"who are you?" asked the ghost.

"The King of the grim reapers," Blake said. "and my son did not kill you!"

"Lancelot Blake Valentine Alexander-Drax," Reynard dressed in a police sergeant's uniform said,

"The Enchanter, I know his name!" said the detective on the case.

"He's a suspect in the case," said Reynard.

"Why? He's nice and he helps the police!" said the detective.

"Only when it suits him," Reynard said, "he's protecting the Necromancer."

"Is that why there is an all points bulletin out on him and he's in hiding?" asked the detective.

"Yes!" Reynard said.

Lance heard a voice behind him call his name he span around.

"What?" he asked seeing Blake.

"Here to gloat at the depths I've fallen?" Lance asked.

"No I want help you," said Blake.

"You want to help me? I am a murderer!" said Lance.

"I know but not in the second case!" said Blake, "The victim didn't know you! I interrogated his ghost even showed him your picture."

"What did he say?" asked Lance.

"The killer was a man in jeans and a red raincoat," said Blake here is a sketch of him which I did from the last memory of the victim.

"I know that face," Lance said.

"You know him?" Blake asked.

"He's on Fate's list of people to die at my hand!" Lance said.

"How do you know a face in a list?" Blake asked.

A folder appeared in Lance's hand.

"His file! You aren't the only one who does paperwork." Lance said and handed over the folder to Blake who read the file.

"That's him!" said Blake.

"Somehow he knew he was on my radar!" Lance said.

"He wants you out of the way so you don't kill him!" Blake said.

"He's a serial killer who got away with his crimes that's why he was on my list!" Lance said.

"I see," Blake said.

"I think he is due to have a visit from Mortimer and the Necromancer!" Blake said.

"To put the fear of God in him!" Lance said.

"Yes, no one is afraid of Blue Midnight and the Enchanter," Blake said.

Later elsewhere the killer was processing a murdered victim for disposal.

"I am the grim reaper here to take your soul!" a grim reaper said in a voice like a dying man reaching one boney arm out to the killer.

"What?" said the killer turning around to see the reaper Mortimer walking towards him,

"Repent or die!" Mortimer said acting scary.

the killer pulled the knife he was cutting the cadaver up with up and pointed it at Mortimer, who laughed like a madman.

"You can't kill a skeleton with a knife!" said the reaper.

"What the-" said the killer feeling a sharp thing pointed in his back.

"Boo!" Lance said.

"What do you want and don't say, my soul! You sound like a church!" said the killer.

"We are here to see that you pay for your murders!" said Lance.

"Um! What murders?" said the killer nervously fully aware they saw his latest victim.

"You framed me, for one of your murders!" Lance said darkly.

"The Necromancer?" asked the killer.

"Who else!" Lance said and then laughed like a madman.

Suddenly the killer found himself at the police station surrounded by the police. The sergeant was eating a sandwich when he saw them.

"Get them!" the sergeant screamed.

"Confess!" Lance ordered he had his sword in the killer's back.

"This is the true killer of the second murdered victim attributed to the Necromancer!" Mortimer hissed.

"What?" said Reynard.

"I interrogated the ghost of his victim he fingered him!" The reaper said.

"Why is there a reaper here?" asked Reynard.

"I am here to clear his name," said the reaper.

"What have you done to Lance Alexander your lover?" asked Reynard.

"Oh please! I'm married! He's just a friend, who wanted to clear my name, he knew you'd start throwing wild accusations, I told him about my victim so he lied and defended me!" Lance snapped, "How did you know you were on my list?"

"A ghost told me!" said the killer.

"Why is he covered with blood," asked Reynard of the killer.

"He was cutting up his latest victim when we caught him he's a serial killer," Mortimer said and thought "I'll deal with that ghost."

"Who is he?" Reynard asked.

A folder materialized in Reynard's hand.

"The list of crimes of this killer," Lance said.

"Arrest that man, ignore the grim reaper, he's dead," Reynard said, "The reapers are harmless, more bark than bite, they are vultures around souls! What I want to know is why a reaper would help the killer, the Necromancer even if he was innocent? Who are you to him!"

Mortimer disappeared into thin air.

"Bye, Dad," said Lance in Mortimer's mind.

"Arrest, those Murderers!" Reynard snapped pointing at Lance and the killer.

"See you around," said Lance disappearing into thin air.

"Whose that guy," asked the Enchanter walking in the room moments later with Blue Midnight.

"What did we miss?" Blake asked.

"The Necromancer and a grim reaper just apprehended a serial killer!" Reynard said, "We haven't clue where to find his victims we'll need you to talk to your friend Mortimer the Grand Reaper to find the bodies."

"A reaper was with him? If I know my friend Mort, he'll have hell to pay if Mort catches him he doesn't like the Necromancer, right son," said Blake beaming.

"Yes they hate each other!" said Lance smiling.

"Why are you blocking your minds?" Reynard said, "Why aren't you two fighting you are worse than Blake and Max none stop fighting what started the love in, oh! Come on! You hate each other."

"What is wrong with you I love my children," Blake said, "I don't agree with them sometimes."

"Same with me, even if he's got a paperwork fetish I don't understand I love my Dad he's the best Dad," Lance said.

"What are you, changelings? Come to my office I'll have to investigate this." Reynard said.

Blue Midnight and the Masked Chicken

Oh darn!" Max who was in disguise in a tux and mask said. Blake was disguised too he wore a mask and blue tux.

Blake looked at Max confused.

"Is anything wrong, Blake asked.

"Can you please take me to hell!" asked Max.

"take you to what?" Blake king of the grim reapers laughed.

"Blue Midnight and the Sun King this is exciting lets go fight crime!" A man in a yellow chicken suit with a mask said like they made his life.

"Ok, I'll race you there," said Blake seeing the chicken,

"Can I join you!" the chicken enthused said.

"Oh hello Masked Chicken, Nice to see you again," Lied Max, all the real super heroes like Max and Blake dreaded meeting this super zero the Masked Chicken. He wanted to be a hero and chaos followed him. He was a sorcerer who chose not to use magic.

"The King and I were going to-" Blake said stopping speaking because the chicken was being beaten by a old lady he crossed the road with.

"Why did the chicken cross the road!" laughed Max.

"I wanted to catch that bus leave me alone you Idiot!" she screamed as she was dragged away from the bus it left when she was taken across the road nearly under a car.

"Max we better save him from the old lady," Blake said. Although he was much older than the old lady by 2000 years yet he looked 25 like all his race.

Max and Blake ran over to them.

"We'll deal with this chicken, Madam," Blake said dragging the chicken away from the old lady who was still hitting him.

"Thank you Blue Midnight, that chicken made me miss my bus," she said happy to see him taken away. Max and Blake walked him away..

"Let's go for a coffee Chicken, King," said Blake,

"Yes," Max said realizing that Blake meant to get the chicken out of trouble.

"We are going on the lamb," said the chicken gleefully.

Blake and Max looked at each other saying oh god in the others head.

"Look a good cafe, my wife, Angela loves this place," Blake said.

taking them in to a cafe.

"What do you want, Blue Midnight and friends," a waitress asked when they'd been seated.

"Latte," Max said, although he was a vampire he did eat and drink normal stuff as well as blood.

"Long Macchiato," Blake said,

the chicken was busy looking at the other guests for crimes being committed, but, none were.

"what does the chicken want!" asked the waitress not sure why he was dressed as a chicken and why he needed a mask as he was dress in a chicken suit.

"I am on the Lamb!" said the chicken not listening.

Blake grinned embarrassed.

"Get him a milkshake with a long straw," Max said.

She left them to get the orders.

"Chicken," Max said, " stop looking for crimes we are here to sit and drink,"

"Who do you think Midnight and I are Batman and Robin?" asked Max.

"No Mandrake and Sailor Moon!" the chicken said.

"What!" Blake snapped, "Not Tuxedo Mask?"

"No he just throws flowers! Your magic warriors!" said the chicken.

"Magic warriors!" laughed Blake.

"Crime fighters!" the chicken said.

Blake couldn't stop laughing he saw himself as a super hero and sorcerer.

"Max we are magic warriors!" Blake laughed.

"Blake calm down everyone thinks you're mad!" Max said glaring at Blake.

"He's a coroner," said Max, " I'm the son of a Policeman! we help if we must."

"Wasn't he a Canadian Mountie, who rode a horse!" asked the chicken who was very impressed,

"He was a were-wolf too! does that mean you are a werewolf?".

"Yes," Max as if he'd rather not admit it said.

"So you are a vampire, werewolf and an enchanter that's how you can stand the sun!," said the chicken.

Max grunted in reply.

"Why don't you use your powers? you are a sorcerer too" asked Max.

"Oh them! I prefer manual work!" said the chicken.

The chicken made the sugar disappear with his powers.

"Why'd you do that?" Max snapped.

"It is bad for people! Sugar can kill!" said the chicken.

"So can I," Max snapped.

"Calm down Max," Blake said, "I don't need more paper work!"

The waitress came back with their orders.

She saw the sugar disappear and was scared what they'd do to her.

She put the drinks out and ran off without asking if they wanted anything else.

"She thinks we are dangerous," said Blake nervously..

"I thought we could come here without any trouble," Max said frustrated.

Blake looked Mortified.

"I want to die!" Blake said feeling as if everyone was watching him as they were.

"Die later Blake!" Max said, "we don't need to explain why the grim reaper's here and you are dead."

The chicken was enjoying his milkshake too much he was making noises.

"Drink up Blake," said Max who began bolting down his coffee he didn't feel the heat as a native of the sun.

Blake sipped nervously at his coffee.

When all were finished and paid up. Blake and Max left the chicken.

"Good thing we were masked no one will recognize us," Max said laughing. as Blake bought a news paper.

"Batman and Robin of QueensCross, Blue Midnight and the Sun King crack murder by talking to victim's ghost!" the boy Blake bought the paper off shouted.

"Max maybe I am Batman after all!" Blake said.

"No I'm Batman you are Robin!" Max shouted.

"No you're Robin, I'm Batman," Blake said.

We leave them now arguing over who was who!

All I know is they were Blue Midnight and his best friend The Sun King.

A Vampire in a car crash

Max I'm sorry your friend Michael is dead!" I told my friend who was in shock after having a car accident I was the coroner Max wasn't hurt because he was already dead.
"You would be dead too if you weren't a vampire!" I said.
"How do I look doc?" Max who looked a mess asked.
"I'm not going there, fix yourself your a sorcerer, and don't call me doc you aren't bugs bunny!" I told him "get out of that wreck"
"oh right!" max said materializing out of the car when he appeared he looked healthy and was in a clean set of clothes.
"You look better!" I said, "the police want to talk to you!"
"More paper work ," said Max.
"yeah," I said, "paper work!"
"Am I going to jail you think," asked Max.
"Possibly survive and you are guilty. you have that chance," I told him,
Later at his trial.
"Why did you crash" asked the lawyer for the people.

I am Blake Alexander and my life is hell!

I am Blake Alexander and my life is hell!
It all began centuries ago but I won't go there.
I am over 2000 years old I am not human obviously,
I am of an alien sorcerer race but generations were born here on Earth.
"Dr Death another one died in the hospital we need you to tell their family they died," A doctor at the hospital I work said. The call me Dr Death, because I'm the local coroner, "Ok give me the paper work!"
he gave me the paperwork. I knew I would have to deal with the case later as coroner as it said the patient was murdered by a vampire.
"not another vampire killing!" I said. "at least it wasn't the insane Necromancer he leaves a mess!" the doctor replied.
"true and more paper work!" I said. To tell you the truth The Necromancer is my son.
"I have some bad news for you your Gary has died we suspect he was a vampire victim," I told the distraught family of the victim later.
Then I saw him he took my attention from the family totally he was a vampire not just a vampire he was their king.
"Max what the hell are you doing here?" I said aloud,
"I was looking for you," Max said he sounded like there was a problem.
"It's Astra!" Max said. She was his wife and my great granddaughter.
"What is it?" I asked.
"A vampire hunter has her!" Max cried. " Whatever for?" asked the grieving wife. I replied "you don't want to know," and I left with Max.
I spied one of the grim reaper race walk from a room of the hospital.
"more paper work," I mumbled. seeing it. "What?" Max asked.
"just another of my reapers taking a soul," I replied.

I am the king of the reapers but that is only part of my hell.
I'll need to process that poor soul later in the other world.
I will leave you now. You don't need to know how we saved Astra. Enduring is always paid with hell to me.

The Magicians

Good evening Ladies and Gentlemen," a disembodied voice on the stage of a magic show said,
"Abracadabra!" the voice said and the frame of a tall handsome black haired man in a tux and top hat materialized. "I am Blake Fire", a brunette man in a tux and top hat walked on stage "and he Is my assistant Max Starfire!"
"I am your partner grandead!" Max hissed.
"Enough Max! I'll sick a vampire hunter on you and your wife the queen of vampires;" Blake snapped back.
"I thought you loved your granddaughter Blake," Max said as he pulled a rabbit out of a hat.
"I do but vampires are a pain in the neck!" Blake snapped as he did a rope trick.
"More Paper work as a coroner with the police and the grim Reaper I suppose!" Max retorted like a barb.
" Actually yes! The paper work is hell!," Blake said pulling a bunch of flowers out of thin air.
"I thought so bureaucrat to the last" said Max laughing.
"Someone has to tidy up the mess you leave behind," Blake said doing a magic trick.
"Well with out us life would be boring," said Max smiling charmingly.
A ghost walked on stage Blake looked frustrated.
"What the hell this place isn't haunted! Max is this your work!" Blake snapped,
"No!" Max said confused.
"I heard you spoke to the dead so I came!" said the ghost.
"Great another one what do you want!" Blake grumbled.
"I hear you know the sorcerer Blake Alexander known as Blue Midnight," the ghost said.
"He is him!" Max said.
"That's real magic not a stage trick?" the ghost asked.
"I'm over worked I moonlight as a stage magician!" Blake said,
"I'm busy what do you want!"
"An autograph!" the ghost said.
"Our ghost is an autograph hunter!" Max said laughing.
"You want an autograph?" Blake said skeptically."show me your paper first,"
"He's a bureaucrat to the bone!" Max laughed.
"You have to be!" Blake said reading the fine print he thought might be there.
"I the over signed will not take the undersigned to the other world." read Blake frowning, "I knew it was fishy! He knew who I was he just wanted to haunt his wife"
"How did you know I didn't tell you that!" the ghost said.
"Hey, I'm a sorcerer; I read minds! I've been talking to Max in his head for the whole show; no one in the audience can hear us; and I am a necromancer; I read ghost's minds. I sensed you were here I am hiding you from the audience!" Blake said, "stay there I'll take you for processing when the show finishes."
"How can he hear me?" the ghost asked.
"Oh him he's dead! My friend is a vampire and a sorcerer he is as good as a necromancer!" Blake

explained " and he has a neck fetish!"

"Hey!" Max said offended.

"Just saying it as it is," Blake said.

"Where is the other world anyway?" the ghost asked.

"You are going there it's in his backyard!" Max said.

"His backyard?" the ghost asked.

"Yes it is Elysian my backyard," Blake said." shows done "

Blake walked off stage in to a cupboard and dropped dead out of the cupboard walked the grim reaper to take the ghost to his backyard.

"Bye Mortimer!" said Max to the reaper Mortimer as they left.

www.ingramcontent.com/pod-product-compliance
Lightning Source LLC
Chambersburg PA
CBHW070533130626
46555CB00003B/1396